The Dead of Easter

AN OTHER EARTH STORY 3

The Dead of Easter

AN OTHER EARTH STORY 3

TORY FAVRO

The Dead of Easter
Blood & Chocolate
An Other Earth Story 3

Many thanks to my amazing beta readers! Emma Brown, Ian Gielen and Matthew Jon Smith

Edited by Allison Olbrich - My love and my life. I hope that by my next book your surname has changed to match mine.

Cover Design by Ruth Anna Evans

Interior Design and Typesetting by Steven Pajak (My Hero!)

THE GARDEN

"Motherfucker!" Timmy nearly dropped his carrot as he looked out of the window into the dark garden beyond. Something had moved against the shrubbery at the back fence. He was sure of it.

His mother smacked him in the back of the head and yelled, "Timmy! How many fucking times have I told you to watch that little mouth of yours, Mister?"

He used his back foot to brush his fur back up over his long ears, and mumbled, "More than once?"

"You're goddamned right more than once, and you should have caught on by now. There goes your spinach pudding for dessert!"

Shit, this night was not getting any better. In fact, it was really sucking a big one. *Shut the fuck up, you idiot, before she takes away your console time too.* He ruffled his fur back over his long ears and said in a low voice, "Aw Mom..."

"Don't you 'Mom' me, young man." She nervously looked out of the window at what had got Timmy's attention. The shadows of the garden had turned an ominous dark shade, as though the teenage rabbit's fright had turned off the moonlight.

1

"There's nothing out there. Why did you scare me like that?"

"But there is! I'm sure I saw something. It was like a shadow walking down at the end of the garden, Mom! I promise! I fucking promise!"

Another clip to the back of the head, "You keep that up young man, and you'll end up not eating for a week. A young rabbit needs his food!"

"Yes Mom." Timmy sheepishly looked down at the table.

"And how do you think your father's gonna react when he knows you're swearing the way you are? He'll be as angry at you as he is with your brothers and sisters!"

"Sorry Ma, please don't tell him." Fucking hell, he really didn't want his father to know.

"I've got half a mind to young man. We've got quite the reputation to uphold as you know!

Timmy didn't argue. He knew his mother was right. They did have quite the reputation to live up to, and it didn't help that his father was none other than the freaking Easter Bunny, but the thing was, Timmy and his brothers and sisters all over Easterland had different moms with different rules except for the one set by Dad.

Dad's name was Buck and he liked to –

A LONG WALK HOME

F uck!

Buck lifted his head up off the bar.

Where the fuck was he meant to be tonight? This was part of the problem with being the Easter Bunny. They didn't turn off the tab at the bar. After all, they knew where the chocolate came from. He was the damn Easter Bunny after all, but that still wouldn't get him out of trouble with the Missus. It was just a matter of which Missus he was meant to be with tonight.

Kids! Kids! Kids!

At times, it felt like they were all over the fucking place. He loved them all equally, but he certainly had favourites. *I think that's one of the things about being a parent* Buck thought to himself. *We pretend that we like them but we sometimes don't, and for sure some of them also make our lives a lot harder too.*

The Barman looked at him sympathetically and with a little bit of jealousy.

"Not good, sir. You are requested at Cabbage Hill."

"Thanks, Ted," Buck rubbed at his one bloodshot eye. It wasn't myxomatosis, but sure as hell felt like it.

"I've called you a cab, Buck."

"Forget that, I've got time to walk." Buck got up a little unsteadily and checked his watch. It wasn't the end of the world that he was a bit late but he needed enough time to clear his head before he got home. He had a good lady up there at Cabbage Hill and loved her dearly. She wasn't needy and she understood their relationship. It was hard being married to the Easter Bunny, especially when you were not the only one he called wife. It didn't really matter how late he was when he turned up as long as he did. He always made sure he did.

He hit the road and heard the door to the bar close behind him, the door smacking against the frame a couple of times before it locked. Something seemed off in Easterland tonight. There was a kind of tension that filled the air. A couple more shots would've got rid of that, but the carrot vodka wasn't hitting the mark the way it should.

"Same time tomorrow," he said to the building, tipping an imaginary cap. There was a chill in the air and Buck knew that a brisk hop would both clear his head and warm him up.

He hit his head on the sign just outside and fell to the ground, feeling sheepish. No one built signs with a six foot bunny in mind. He glanced about, the street was empty.

Good.

As he stumbled along the road, he dug his heels into the dirt of the gutter. Fuck, it was cold outside tonight! That was one of the things he noticed since the change, even though it was so long ago. Being bigger didn't always come with its benefits. He felt the cold, he needed special clothes, and he felt like he was always hungry.

Whistling out loud made the trip a little easier, though being shitfaced didn't. Stumbling from side to side of the small road, he was aware that he was not going anywhere quickly, and gave out a little laugh.

Ha!

It was good to be alive! In fact, the entirety of Easterland was lucky to be alive after the event of the Pulse. A cataclysmic event, its origins still unknown. It affected most of the human world, which he'd been out in over the last few years, delivering eggs to the humans that had managed to survive so far.

Fuck, that made it sound dramatic. It wasn't as though they were in danger of being wiped off the face of the planet, but the dead now walked the Earth (things of science-fiction were becoming science fact), including an entire land of rabbits and forest animals, who now interacted with technology and did all the other dumb things that humans liked to do. Oh, and delivered chocolate throughout multiple dimensions.

Nearby, a truck gently tooted its horn and Buck got off the side of the road. It wouldn't pay to end up on a supermarket tray this close to Easter. No siree bob, no good at all. The draft from the truck pulled Buck back toward the road again, and he staggered forward, being caught in its slipstream.

Buck was pulled forward by his ears, and for a brief moment, he thought he was flying. Then he *was* flying, face first into the dirt. The booze took care of most of the pain and he spat out the grit that was caught in between his big teeth.

Gotta get home, Buck thought to himself.

It had been a big day and his wife would be understanding, but not if he came home covered in blood and gunk. Buck patted the back of his jeans, and felt the reassuring shape of his pistol. Yes, he may have been in Easterland. And yes, he may have been the motherfucking Easter Bunny, but he was always strapped.

In the hedge nearby, some small, red eyes glared at him. There was a whistling sound low to the ground and the scurrying of little feet. Buck whipped around, the sound attracting his attention, but there was nothing to be seen.

Shake it off bitch, he said to himself and kept on walking.

Not far to go now before the rise of Cabbage Hill came into

view. It was more of an incline rather than a hill, but the way he felt, it may as well have been Cabbage Mountain. Grumbling to himself, the Easter Bunny put one foot in front of the other and continued up the street.

CHICKEN SHIT

Back at the hedge where we saw the red eyes just moments ago, five small figures congregated on the front lawn of a house.

"Is this it? Is this it?" one asked the other.

"Yep, sure is."

"So do we put on the masks?"

"If you really want to, but I don't see the point. You know they don't see us as individuals."

"Yeah, it will be fun. I'm going to."

"Well, if you're going to, I am too! Peep!"

There were other nods of agreement and the five adolescent chickens pulled rubber masks over their faces. It may have been wishful thinking, but they were the masks of a rooster from a long forgotten cartoon. Disguises intact, they snuck around the side of the house, the moonlight casting long shadows from their little bodies.

One stumbled into the other, causing them both to fall, the others laughed.

"Too much noise, dickheads, he'll wake up!"

This was gonna be a great prank.

One of the chickens in this group by the name of Hank, well, this was his dad's house, and he didn't live with his dad, but they had the greatest fun playing pranks on each other. His friends wanted in on it, so the idea was they would sneak inside, get up to the second floor where his dad, a heavy sleeper, should be in bed. Then, they would put balloons, filled with water, all around his butt and wait for him to roll on them, thinking he'd pissed the bed.

That was the general idea. Anyhow, the back door was locked and Hank didn't have his key.

The group continued around the house, trying not to make too much noise. In the meantime, something fluttered hard against the front door. Scaring the shit out of them. Literally making them shit themselves. They sheepishly looked down at the five nuggets on the ground, trying not to laugh. They would have to clean that up before Hank's dad saw it or he wouldn't hear the end of it.

He pointed at the ground.

"We have to get rid of that, or Dad will think that we're chickenshit."

They all laughed and then listened. Carefully.

The weird noise was still coming from inside the house, like something was thumping around blindly in the dark, with no idea of what it was doing or where it was going,

"I think I'm gonna go home," one of the guys at the back said.

"We all promised each other that we'd do this together," Hank said. "Get some balls."

You know I've got them, they're in my back," came the reply.

"For now," Hank said, pretending to be menacing.

Eventually the noise inside the house subsided and it sounded like the front door slammed.

"I bet it was Dad fucking with us," he said more to himself than the others.

Those loud sounds weren't like anything he was used to hearing around here. After the back door disappointment, checking the side door wasn't any better; it was locked too. It all seemed too quiet, too still now after the cacophony of only a moment ago. Now it felt like the shadows of the house were waiting for them to come inside to smother them in its warm embrace. He knew he shouldn't have been eating chocolate this late at night before sneaking around in the dark. It played all sorts of tricks with his mind.

"I'll see if I can get in through my bedroom window."

The rest of them looked at Hank in admiration and fright. There was a trellis covered with vines going up the back of the house, cut away where Hank's window was. The chicken climbed quickly up the trellis.

Now, don't overthink this, he thought and tested the windows with his wings, but he couldn't get them open. He made a clucking sound of disappointment and climbed back down.

"Fuck, that would've made things a lot easier," he said. "Maybe we need to call this off."

The others agreed. It seemed like a bit of fun earlier. Now, because of how late it was, and how dark it was in this backyard, with all the lights off, it felt wrong. There was a crash at the end of the yard, and a long shadow moved, casting itself along the back lawn. The chickens looked at each other and made their way quickly back to the front. Just as they were about to leave, Hank looked back and saw the front door of the house swinging open. With a trembling wing, he pointed back at it.

"Was the door open before?"

"I don't know, but I've had enough. I'm heading home, but first maybe you should go in and check on your dad. I'll come with you," said Ernie. He was Hank's best friend, and to be honest, he was the reason why the other three were even here. They had been sleeping over at Ernie's house, and he came up with the idea of pulling a prank on Hank's dad.

Hank nodded. He was glad for the company. Something was wrong. He just couldn't put his wingtip on what it was.

The other three said their goodbyes and scrambled away up the street, stopping every now and then to peck up the worms that were poking their heads up from the lawns in the moist grass. Soon the three were gone, and Ernie turned to Hank.

"Alright buddy, let's check it out."

They approached the front door, and it readily became apparent why there had been so much noise. The door frame was splintered, and the door swung back open, purely because there was no longer a locking mechanism to hold it in place. This wasn't good. It made a creaking sound that set Hank's egg tooth on edge like the scraping of claws on a blackboard at school. The math teacher, a grumpy fox by the name of Master Silas, ran his claws down such a board to get their attention.

Hank reached out to steady the wobbling door and pulled his wing away in disgust.

"It's fucking sticky. There's something on it."

There was a weird smell coming from the house, one that neither of them liked. Hank stepped past his friend and noticed something on the floor. Something had spilled. He still couldn't figure out what the smell was, but he didn't like it. The house was dark, and even though familiar, the shadows became their own monsters, threatening to reach out and grab the two kids, to pull the two chickens inside them, never to be seen again.

Down the hallway, the ticking of the clock echoed like a whisper of doom. The staircase was to the right, and there was something on the walls there as well. One of the banisters was broken. He didn't want to make a sound, but he had to, in order to make sure his dad was okay.

He called out, in a quavering little voice, "Dad?"

No answer.

There was a sound upstairs though. Maybe Dad had gone to the bathroom. Hank didn't care any more about the fact that they were there to do something on the sly. He would give anything even for his dad to be yelling at him for being out this late at night, and probably giving his mother a heart attack.

"DAD!" Hank called louder this time, still nothing.

It had gone quiet upstairs, and that made it even worse. They creeped up, trying not to get their wings caught up in whatever the hell it was that was smeared all over the place. Hank peaked around the corner, not seeing anything. Some of the doors were open, some were closed. He was more fearful of the ones that were open. His dad was big on shutting doors for rooms that weren't in use and that even included his own when he was staying with his mother. He had hated when they divorced but as he got older he understood why.

That's why it kind of freaked him out that his dad must've opened up the door to his bedroom.

Why was he in there? What was he looking for?

Hank hoped he didn't find the copy of Busty Hen magazine he had hidden under his mattress. He wasn't ready for those questions. He wasn't sure he had answers for them. He gulped, made his way quietly along, and peeked into his bedroom.

There was nothing there. Other than his bedding that had been pulled away from the mattress, piled on the floor. He breathed a sigh of relief. The mattress itself was still in place, which meant those delicious hens were still there for him to visit another time.

Creeping back out of the room, he saw Ernie checking the cleaning cupboard. Hank wasn't sure why, it was a small cupboard, but he guessed it made Ernie feel better that he was helping. The towels didn't jump out, nor did they attack. The detergents stayed where they were, glaring with hatred from the shelves. Hank made a little clucking noise with his beak, and turned around, nearly falling over as his father leaned against his door and loomed over him, but he could see at a glance something was seriously wrong.

"Dad?"

Hank's dad stumbled forward from his bedroom, where the smell was coming from. Overwhelmingly, the stench of rusty metal made Hank puke. He took several steps back from his dad, who was approaching with wings out glaring at him.

Super weird.

"Dad, are you okay? What the fuck?"

In the background he could hear his wings flapping as the chickens went into a panic. There was no other way downstairs, and effectively, they were trapped in the hall. Why was he so scared? Why was his dad acting so weird? He took a step forward, and that's when his father also stepped forward, his features visible in the moonlight, half of his cheek torn out. Feathers on his chest had been ripped out, and what remained were scuffed and stained with blood from the wounds.

But the worst part was his eyes.

They didn't look right.

The normal bright little beads of light were dulled.

"Are you sick? Are you okay? I'll call the police."

Hank started to reach for his smartphone and his father bobbed down and pecked him hard on top of his head. Hank felt dazed, and his feathers twitched. His vision blurred, and he felt a long talon holding his leg down. He twitched and kicked, and another talon stepped onto his chest, piercing his flesh. He started to smell the scent he detected downstairs then he realized it was coming from him. It was blood. His teenage wings fluttered uselessly against the carpet and hit the sides of the walls of the hallway, making a creepy, scraping noise. All the more magnified by the otherwise quiet room. Despite the labored breathing, his dad was utterly silent.

"No! Dad! No! It's your son, it's me, it's Hank."

But whatever it was that he used to be called, Dad was no longer there. The huge rooster loomed over the top of his child, spreading his shattered wings, ignoring the broken bones, or possibly not even feeling them any more, and the zombie rooster tore out the throat of his son, feasting on the flesh and blood that poured from the wound. Shaking his head as he tore, crunched, and ate; the giblets flying all over the place, splattering photos of Hank's family at a happier time.

The zombie didn't care. It was all too preoccupied with what was on the ground in front of it to be looking at happy incubator photos.

At the far end of the hallway, Ernie pushed himself against the wall and wished that he was anywhere but here. He put his wings over his eyes and tried to cover his ear holes, but all he could hear was the scraping noise of Hank's dad stumbling through the thick carpet toward him.

Slowly, he lowered his little wing tips and, despite knowing better, was shocked to see Hank fumbling ahead toward him. Maybe it was the dark. Maybe it was the shock. To be honest, we're never going to know because the dead don't speak, do they? If anything, we can take a little solace that, in the last few moments of his incredibly short life, his killer was Hank, and as his best friend ripped him apart, everything went black.

A few moments later, he got back up again, and the three stumbled about the house until eventually the noises in the neighbourhood waking up in alarm and panic drove them outside, looking for fresh meat.

TEA FOR YOU, TEA FOR ME

"Tea Boss?"

"Fuck yes!"

The March Hare smashed his paw down on the table, making the teacup rattle. The noise was unexpected, startling the two bodyguards standing behind him. Known as the Armadillo Brothers, they were certainly some of the toughest creatures in Easterland and other dimensions and made for an excellent protection detail. One was Max and the other was Reggie, but to be honest, he had no idea which was which.

In the small security room, the wall was covered with control panels and screens. Images of what was happening outside flashed across them. The chaos was spreading even outside the mall they were in, but they were as ready as they were going to be. The March Hare's boss had sent them everything well in advance. It had been hard sneaking about for months, but the March Hare had finally gotten the cameras set up throughout Easterland. Then it had been a waiting game. The March Hare wasn't very good at patience, it was not a virtue, as far as he was concerned.

Throughout the land, he could see fires starting, and it filled the

Hare with glee. He hated this place for a number of reasons, not the least of which was the fact that he should've been running the place. Well, it looks as though that was about to change. It meant that he'd be calling the shots as long as he managed to avoid destroying it entirely. He snorted with laughter, accidentally putting a tooth into his lip. He felt the blood trickle back into his mouth, the pain immediate.

"Oh you motherfucker!"

"Yes, boss?"

One of the brothers spoke up. The March Hare thought it might've been Reggie. He knew they fucking hated this detail but the money was really good. They weren't from Easterland but picked up the job off the dark web and the money had appeared in their accounts pretty quickly. The client pretty soon proved himself to be a fucking psychopath. Sure, Easterland wasn't their scene, but they didn't question why he wanted to destroy the place. *Not their problem* was their mantra, *not their problem*. Compared to some of the stuff that they'd done, this was a walk in the park.

"Nothing, nothing. It's working, it's actually working", the March Hare said excitedly, getting to his feet. He was really tall and towered over the top of the Armadillo Brothers. His twitching and erratic movements constantly making them both reach for their pistols. The brothers were convinced that at some point, he'd make them shoot him purely as a reflex action simply by twitching the way he did.

"That's great, boss."

The March Hare settled back down in his seat. Why hadn't he thought of this a long time ago? It was simple and elegant. Well, to be honest, it was bloody and terrible, but it would get the job done; and it was so easy to do. Just get a box truck, fill it with some live bait in the human world, and make sure there was a ramp for the zombies to come up and chow down. Steal said truck, of course, from the Easterland compound or follow one really closely so that it bypassed the forcefield and drive it back in easy peasy, lemon squeezy, though he had nearly undone everything when he opened the truck back up only to find that the undead stood closer to the opening than he thought.

He giggled to himself at the thought, especially that part. These two idiots had stayed in the car, not wanting any part of the start of his revolution. Oh well, if you want something done properly, do it yourself?

Then it was just a matter of sitting back and letting the undead do their thing. He had missed the first attack, there were no cameras in that area. Stupid, stupid stupid, he thought, as he struck himself in the head, a little bit too hard. He laughed again. By the end of this, Easterland would be a swarming mess of blood and fur and then he would be in charge of things. Fuck this place and especially fuck the Easter Bunny.

He settled back in the reclining chair, unwrapping a chocolate bar. Its creamy dairy milk stared back at him, the raisins in it taunting him. He took a bite, relishing the dopamine hit. He couldn't wait till this job was over and he handed the chocolate ingredients to the guy who had contracted him. Then he'd whack the rabbit. Maybe he would whack the rabbit earlier than that? It all sounded kind of wonderful.

The March Hare took another big bite, the rich sweetness mixing in with the iron taste of his own blood. A smile spread across his face.

Delicious!

WHO'S THAT CREEPIN' ROUND MY FRONT DOOR?

Timmy tossed and turned as he tried to get to sleep under his quilt. It was a cold night and his pelt wasn't doing anything to help keep him warm. Occasionally he would hear odd noises that drew his attention back out the window. Just like earlier, he could've sworn there was something out there in the backyard moving about. It got to the point that he had gone back downstairs twice more, to the irritation of his mother who was trying to keep his father's food warm. The phone message from his dad had told them both that he was on his way home. Tim was a little bit pissed. He liked the nights with his father and knew that Buck had other kids that he had had to spend time with as well, but this was meant to be his special night with his dad, and his dad was running so late that he had to go to bed without seeing him.

Dad would be up in time for breakfast and at least maybe he could walk him to school.

It was getting harder to go back to sleep. The anticipation was too much, and it didn't help that he stayed up way beyond his bedtime playing online with his friends. There was a sound again. He cracked the window open, just slightly, not wanting to attract any real attention, and didn't turn on the light. He put his rabbit nose to the window and sniffed so that his sense of smell might tell him just what the heck was going on, twitching with all the noise. In the distance, there was a red glow. What was going on there? And the smell told him that something was burning, not like the good burning smell when they had the big fires to clear some of the forest where trees were falling down, but he could smell a weird chemical scent of paint and things that you used to make houses. It was a house fire and it raced through the streets of Cabbage Hill, cops and fire trucks doing their best to take charge of the situation, though even as his little face looked out the window he could see more red glows appearing. It was really weird. None of the forest was on fire, though that would happen soon. They lived in the forest after all, it looked as though people were deliberately setting fire to their homes. Which didn't make any sense. The smell was making him feel sick, and he shut the door as well as the window to try to block it out some. He snuggled back down into his bed, and that's when he heard a commotion downstairs.

Come on Buck, please get home, Mrs Bunny thought to herself. She, too, could hear all the sounds Timmy kept hearing bringing him down to annoy her with. It was bad enough that her own imagination was running away. Let alone her son who she knew was playing online way too long, coming down with his own guesses at just what was happening. Something was wrong and Buck was not picking up the phone any more.

She just hoped that he wasn't asleep in a gutter or worse, caught up in just whatever the fuck was happening out there. She'd given up on keeping his dinner warm, a couple of hours ago. It would serve him right to come home to a cold meal, though to be honest she would give anything to get the stove going and cook him something fresh while he sat there in front of her. Absently she got a fresh pot of carrots and washed out some spinach. He was easy to cook for, a good provider, not that he really had any excuse to be anything but considering he was the Easter Bunny. She was proud of the role that they had to play and the happiness that they were able to spread throughout the world and that plenty of other bunnies also helped.

There was a crash against the front door and she thought that she could hear glass falling from the little panes on the left and right of it, just a little tinkle. It was more the impact of the door that startled her and knocked her out of her reverie and she glanced down toward the entrance. Normally, the security light would turn on outside, illuminating whoever the guest was. Nothing, though, maybe it was broken. She gently hopped down the hallway as Buck's meal bubbled on the stove. There was a sound outside. Something at the door? She was not sure. She heard a claw scrape and breathed a sigh of relief.

The next door neighbor had recently lost his wife. A gentle brown bear, she had been having him over quite often for meals to help him cope with his loss. His breathing permeated through the door and the smell of his fur helped calm her down. It was a known something she identified with normal life; sure there was an odd smell behind it, possibly from the fires and other bad things that seem to be happening in the neighbourhood this evening.

"Boris!" Mrs Bunny swung the door open to her friend. The brown bear was standing upright, knocking out the security light with the top of his head. It wasn't the first time, and it wouldn't be the last. Blood trickled down the fur, over his dark black eyes and over his nose, which oddly enough didn't seem very wet. "

Are you okay?" She asked as a massive paw swung forward and the claws tore through her ears which flopped forward. She made a high-pitched scream of pain and fell backwards into the house. The brown bear stumbled, tripping over the door frame and landed on top of her, breaking her leg. Adrenaline coursed through her body, and she scrambled to try to get out from under him, eventually kicking him in the face. He didn't seem to notice but it moved him just enough for her to pull her leg out. She could feel the different parts of the broken bone trying to go in separate directions and she screamed again, pulling herself up on her one good leg. She placed herself against one of the walls and frantically hopped away, knocking down pictures of the family from their frames as she did so.

"Timmy! Hide!"

In the hallway, they had a telephone stand, just one of the short ones with the retro phone on it as a decoration. No one used them nowadays, but her cell phone was down in the lounge room. One of the wooden legs caught her foot and sent her tumbling into the opposite wall smashing vases and glassware, the shards getting caught up in her fur and shredding it. Covered in dead flowers, blood and water, Mrs Rabbit spun about in time to see Boris now on all fours lumbering toward her.

Foam and blood lathered his jaws, and she tried to back away but the wall prevented her escape. The smell that was outside now was coming from within and she knew that her kitchen was on fire. It seemed like a short amount of time. It seemed to play out in slow motion, the dinner that she had been preparing had set the wall ablaze just behind the stove. *I should've turned off the stove* was her last thought as her rib cage cracked as the creature that used to be her next door neighbor stepped on it without preamble and dove his snout into her guts.

Powerful jaws opened, and closed like a mindless machine and drained the life from her small body. She hoped that her son was safe, that was a very short lived thought, she was too busy dying. Boris feasted upon his neighbor; another source of food. His dead nose twitched and his ears curved forward. He wasn't capable of thought anymore, not in the way that you would expect. He was aware that something living was upstairs, something to eat. He lumbered over the top of Mrs Bunny crushing her head, which was probably the kindest thing he did all evening. Her body gave one final death rattle as the nerve endings ceased to function, and she was not going to get back up. One last twitch and her little body was done for.

HIDE

pstairs, Timmy heard his mom screaming. It was a sound that he had never heard before. Sure, he'd heard her yelling most of the time at him, but not in pain. Not like this. Something was terribly wrong and he was scared shitless. Something big was in the house. It sounded like Mr Boris from next door. But by the weird noises being made by him, whatever they were, he wasn't keen to find out.

Come on Dad, where are you? Please get home. He fumbled for his cell phone tucked under his pillow and with shaking paws he swiped up and nothing happened. The room was too dark for Face ID so Timmy adjusted it so that the moonlight hit him through the window and tried again, and that worked. He spoke to the phone. It would understand him.

"Call Dad, call Dad," but his voice was trembling, too much for the technology to do what it was meant to do. As he found his father's phone number, he could smell fire downstairs. The phone rang as it connected. He was amazed that it had service sometimes. When there were fires, the exchanges got overloaded, and he couldn't call his friends, but he could hear the phone ringing.

"Son?" The reassuring voice of his dad came over the phone. There was a hell of a lot of commotion behind him.

"Dad, where are you?"

"I'm just coming up the hill, son. I'll be there in just a moment. I'm going as quick as I can."

"Dad can you go quicker than that please, there's something really wrong. Mom is yelling downstairs, and it sounds like Mr Boris is in the house. She's told me to hide."

"If she told you to hide then goddamn well do so. You remember how to get into the closet room?"

"I think so. I'll go there now."

Timmy opened the door to the closet and moved the shoes out. Behind, there was a button that opened the small cavity that they could access from the separate bedrooms. It was essentially a small storage room reinforced by Dad with tins of preserved vegetables and water in there.

"Okay I'm in there."

"Before you shut the door, make sure you pull everything back so that if someone's looking for you, it won't appear suspicious."

Timmy pulled back the rack of clothes and it swung into place against the wall effectively hiding his location.

"Okay, done."

"Good. What's that noise?"

Timmy's voice, trembling, said "I think he's outside my room."

KNOCK KNOCK! I'M DEAD!

The door splintered and a guttural roar filled the small bedroom. "I'm scared Dad."

"It's okay boy, I'll be there soon."

"I'm really scared Dad, I think Mom's dead."

There was a slight pause and Buck replied, "I'm on my way. I love you and I'm on my way. Be quiet, don't move. I'll be there just as soon as I can."

Timmy slid the wall panel shut and curled himself into a ball at the far end of the room. Dad would be here soon, meanwhile, in the dark several feet from the trembling rabbit, Boris floundered about. His undead senses overflowed with confusing information. He could smell something living. He thought he could hear something living, but he couldn't see anything living in this room. His undead brain processing through synapses starting to decay, dictated that there was something in the room, he just had to find it. What remained of his primordial bear senses and their ability to forage for food in the most hostile environments kicked in, and with his massive strength, he started to pull apart the bedroom.

Buck ran up the street, just as fast as he could. At the top of the hill was a little house he knew well, one of many little houses he knew well, but it was filled with two people that he loved. He could see fire on the lower floor and that immediately set him running even faster. He pulled the pistol from the back of his jeans and pulled back the slide action taking the safety off making sure his paw was not on the trigger and raced up the steps. In the dim light of the hallway, he could see a crumpled figure on the ground, whilst overhead, there was a terrible, smashing noise. He paused briefly and knelt down beside the shattered remains of his wife.

"I'm so fucking sorry my love."

She did not stir as the sound above continued. He made his way down the hole and into the kitchen. The corner of the room was burning, he didn't care about the house but he also didn't want his son burning over the top of his head as the flame spread. He quickly threw the emergency blanket over the top and dusted the rest with the chemical washer bolted to the end of the bench. On the counter lay one of his wife's sharp knives which he picked up for good measure too, and with a weapon in each hand, he went up the steps slowly and cautiously. Whatever up there was big, really big, it smelled like his neighbour but as though something was really off.

The sound in the bedroom was still loud, Timmy thought. Mr Boris had finished wrecking everything in there. It was quiet for just a moment, and he thought the big bear was about to leave his room when all of a sudden in his hand, his cell phone vibrated and a notification sound filled the darkened room.

Oh fuck, fuck he thought to himself, trying to push the phone back into his stomach to muffle the sound, not thinking to turn off the volume. He heard the big brown bear move about clumsily in the wreckage of his room and the closet door was smashed apart and huge claws came through the wall of his hidey hole. Another hit and the massive head of the bear poked through snapping and drooling saliva and blood. His movements flicking it about the walls like cheaply applied special effects makeup in a horror movie.

Buck heard the increased noise and raced up, seeing Boris with his head sticking through the wall of his son's panic room. There was something wrong with the bear. There was blood all over him, but didn't know what from and didn't care at this point. He kicked both feet into the bear, toppling him onto one side, pulling his head away from the hole in the wall. Boris stumbled backward, the new sensory information telling him that something bigger to eat was nearby. The undead part of his brain prioritizing that food information and whirled about and saw the huge thing that kicked him. It was all reflex response and nothing to do with conscious thought.

Buck looked at his old neighbour with fury and fear. The beast stumbled forward with a huge swipe of his paw, just missing him. Buck jumped backwards then dove under one of the swinging arms, punching Boris in the solar plexus, and then head-butting him in the chin with a powerful upward jump. The effect on the bear was next to nothing. He stood back a little, then came forward.

Again, Buck slid along the ground between the bears legs and got up behind him. Whatever the hell was going on, this wasn't Boris any more. This was something weird, and it was something that had killed his wife, and was trying to destroy his son. Buck emptied two shots into the centre mass of his neighbour, where his heart would be. Buck was a good shot. He had to be, especially in his line of work. They were always creeps out during delivery runs, not that he had to unload before, but he made sure he spent enough time down at the range to be a good shot. The big bear didn't even look at the injuries, didn't stop and just kept moving toward him. Once again Buck danced around the flailing arms, getting lucky as he passed through clothing and flesh he flashed out with the knife carving into the thick fur. You could smell and hear intestines, splitting and bowels being perforated, the scent of bear shit overpowering the room. He might as well have been giving Boris a pat for all the damage it did. The thing in front of him was busy as fuck, clumsy as fuck but still moving. Buck ripped the knife back out from the body. For two seconds, he thought about giving another warning shot, but realised he had already pumped two rounds into the creature. Boris dove for the rabbit, throat growling and jaws open Buck emptied the rest of the clip into his head. The bear fell forward. His head rolled and smashed through the wall, his head protruding from the external wall, looking forever outside with its dead, clouded black eyes. Panting, pushing himself back against one of the closet doors, Buck tried to pull himself together.

"Tim... Timmy?"

"Dad?" A quivering little voice replied. His son climbed out from the hole in the wall and into his father's lap in silence, as the pair cried and held each other.

Sometime later during the night, while Timmy was asleep, Buck got up and carefully lifted the remains of his wife onto a sheet. She'd never been a big woman, but her body was so pulverised, it felt as though her mass had been halved. He folded it over her carefully and lifted her gently on their bed, looking out the window the fire had burnt. They'd have to wait. He could see sirens and lights in the distance. He looked away, briefly, catching a glimpse of his own face in the reflection of the window. He was covered with blood from Boris, and he didn't want Timmy to wake up, looking at him like that. He hopped to the bathroom, quickly cleaned up and double checked the kitchen, it was wrecked. Fuck, most of the house was wrecked but it wouldn't burn down while they slept. He dried his face with a towel, smelling the delicate scent of Mrs Bunny's hands on its surface. The sobbing threatened to overwhelm him again, Buck gripped the countertop with his paws until the knuckles went white.

He would get to the bottom of this. He'd known Boris a very long time. The big bear would never have done this of his own voli- tion. Buck knew that something was very wrong. Like, how many times would you have to shoot a brown bear to put it down? He knew it would be a lot. They were nearly unstoppable, especially if the umentaries he'd seen in the human world were true, it took a lot to injure them. He went back upstairs to his son and pulled him close. The teenager muttered something and yelped in his sleep, Timmy cuddled closer to the warm body of his father and nestled back down. Buck thought he felt the boy's body finally relaxing, so with his freehand, he patted about in his jeans pocket, he had friends he could call on, he just hoped that he had service. The phone was heavy and reassuring in his paw. He thumbed a quick dial button.

Pick up you fuckers! Pick up!

THE NORTH POLE (YES THAT ONE)

"Sir? Excuse me, sir?" The roar of the fireplace was almost deafening and the young elf thought he wouldn't be heard. He cleared his throat and the wingtip chair spun around, slowly, revealing a dashingly handsome middle age elf.

The elf took a big puff of a pipe, sipping cognac as the younger elf waited patiently. "Yes, son?"

"There's been communication on the emergency frequency. The person at the other end is talking through a heavily encrypted line. He is asking for you specifically. The link is poor. I've patched it through to your quarters."

"Thank you, old chap, that will be all." The younger elf went to leave, and Rudy the rabid elf, secret weapon of the North Pole and lover of all things rabies motioned with his hand to leave the door open. "Thanks son." The younger elf turned on the communication channel in Rudy's living space and left.

The face of the Easter Bunny filled the screen. The image was grainy as the connection was made.

"Are you paying attention?" Buck said.

"I haven't had that much to drink, but I'd prefer another set of ears." Rudy looked over his shoulder behind the bar, a massive 15 foot reindeer was pouring another round for them. Rudolph looked up, a little bit grumpy. It wasn't easy to pour shots when you don't have hands. It involved a tricky bit of telekinesis to be honest.

The big reindeer brought the drinks over and they switched on the camera at their end. The caller's image was grainy and the room was dark but he knew it was Buck.

"Buck are you okay, what the fuck is going on? Why is the room dark? Is that Timmy?"

Buck breathed a sigh of relief. "Thank fuck I got through to you..."

"There's a massive energy spike in your area." Rudy interrupted, "I don't know how long I will be able to talk for so make it quick."

"You know that shit that went down at the North Pole?" Buck asked.

"Of course I do. Remember, I was ripped to shreds by a thermal detonator at the end of the nonsense that happened here, then I was resurrected by Mike the Alien. Anyway, as you know there is far more detail about that in the first book The Dead of Christmas. Whilst we're not here to make this a plug for the Author, that would be a cheap shot. It might be worth your while picking up The Dead of Christmas when you've got the chance. Do you think something similar is happening there? We have reports throughout multiple dimensions now of such insanity, just like in the second book The Dead of Egypt."

Rudolph moved up next to Rudy, and was examining the outputs on the separate screen, and while Rudy talked, the expression on his face became concerned. The elf looked at his friend.

"We have to get you out of there now. How far away are you from the Rabbit Hole™?"

The Rabbit Hole™, a piece of advanced technology created by the communications officer at the North Pole, yes, that North Pole, let's get it out of the way if there's an Easterland, there is a North Pole with you know who running it, getting toys out to the children just not in the way that you would expect it. Once again details in the first book. You don't need to read it, but you'd probably feel better if you did. A communications officer at the North Pole in any case, an alien by the name of Mike the Alien, he created the Rabbit Hole™ to Easterland. Think of it as a small wormhole big enough to pass things from one location to another, or in extreme circumstances living creatures.

"I'm not at that house tonight, Rudy, but I can get there pretty quickly."

"I would suggest you do, if what we're reading here is accurate this is an evacuation level event. Although I think it's too late already, let me quickly check," he turned and quickly pulled out a keyboard.

"Yes, there are fluctuations to the barriers at the exit of Easterland," the screen came into view as satellites kicked in through powerful cameras, pointing down at the familiar, highway exits that left Easterland. There were fires burning all the way along the border and crumpled trucks, having piled into each other forming a barrier. The front trucks seemingly having collided in mid air. Buck knew that had to be the force field in place keeping humans out except for those with the necessary clearance. The thing is that the forcefield worked the other way, preventing people from coming in, not leaving. He could see the different animals that lived in the land frantically carrying cases and other personal items trying to get out.

The humans knew about the special abilities of those who lived here, but he didn't think they were ready to see them in their day-to-day lives. Certainly not wearing clothes and carrying technology and standing upright and speaking.

Rudy interrupted his thoughts. "There are only a few spaces left in that forcefield before it closes completely, sealing it shut. Someone really wants to fuck you guys up there. We can't reverse engineer the hack, I think you're gonna be stuck in there at the moment, old chap. The Rabbit Hole™ is open. I suggest you wake up Timmy and get him the fuck out of there and I suggest you get out of there too."

The Easter Bunny gently wrestled his son awake. Timmy murmured groggily and looked at his dad's phone.

"Is that Uncle Rudy?"

Rudy looked at him through the screen and smiled.

"It sure is my dear boy, Dad needs to do a lot of things here. You need to go down, get some stuff that you want to keep and come and visit Uncle Rudy with your brothers and sisters. I've got something fun planned for you guys."

Timmy got up and retrieved his backpack, then turned about and looked at his dad, sitting in the shattered remnants of his bedroom.

"Your mom's gone, I'm so sorry son, if only I could've got here earlier."

"It's okay Dad, there's nothing that you could've done, not in time. Mom let Mr Boris in. We didn't know he was so sick."

"I'll be right with you. I just need to finish talking to your Uncle Rudy."

Timmy turned to continue packing. Buck called back to Timmy. The young rabbit glanced at him, his eyes questioning.

"I fucking love you kid."

"I love you too. Is it safe out there?" Timmy asked.

"It is now but we might not be coming back here for some time. I've put Mom in the bedroom if you want to quickly say goodbye." Timmy left the room.

Buck glanced at his phone. The reception was crackly as fuck. He could still make out Rudy and Rudolph looking at him with concern.

"I'll get the kid to the Rabbit Hole™," said Buck, "but there's no fucking way I'm leaving. Make sure you look after him, hell, make sure you look after anyone I send through that fucking hole."

They both nodded, "Of course old friend. Just remember one thing at a time no matter how crazy it gets and being practical, send the children first because if things go pear-shaped and I'm sure they won't, but just in case one of your kids is the next Easter Bunny. Now before you start saying it's more the thought that matters, I know it fucking isn't. Literally one of those children has the genetic bloodline to do what you do. We just haven't figured out who yet so get them through, then help your people."

Rudy consulted the screens, "The problem is all over Easterland now, it's not just near your home," he watched as humanoid shapes made their way after the animals, pulling them to the ground and ripping into them with teeth and claw, the audio was horrific. Rudy did not bother patching it through to Buck. He looked at Rudolph. "It's the same problem isn't it?"

Rudolph nodded.

Timmy, hearing this part of the conversation said, "Problem, what problem?"

"Get the fuck out of there," Rudy said, and just as the line went dead and became nothing but static, Buck heard him say:

"Fucking zombies."

Buck looked at his phone as the secure line died. It was funny he knew he was on his own, but with that communication fading off he felt more stranded. So someone was trying to keep them in? Why? It would be the chocolate, it was always something about the chocolate. Humans and the fucking chocolate, or had someone actually found out the real ingredients kept on site? Zombies in the North Pole? Easterland had avoided it so far. The area was heavily protected by both human agencies and others that he was not allowed to talk about.

Phone cell service was still working in Easterland, and that was a blessing. He hit a number on the speed dial and heard the voice of Betty. She was out of breath and there was commotion about her.

"Buck, thank God, I was so worried about you. It's okay, I'm okay. Are the kids alright?"

"Yes, they're alright"

"Get them to pack just small things then take them down to the basement. Call the other wives and tell them to bring their kids as well."

"It's that bad is it? Betty asked.

"Yes," Buck paused and continued.

"I've spoken to Rudy. When you get down the basement don't be shocked, but I've activated the wormhole, well Rudy has, but he says it won't stay open long, there's a lot of shit going down here and it's all bad. We need to get the kids out. This is a major priority."

There was a pause as Betty absorbed that information.

"Okay", she said, "What about us? The wives?"

"Yes, I feel terrible saying this but I can't keep track of how many kids I have?"

"At last count 23."

"Okay, get the kids through first, the North Pole is waiting for them then very carefully one at a time you girls go through the hole, it may close at any moment."

"Are you with Lucy? How's Timmy?"

"Betty, Lucy's dead. Whatever the fuck this is that's doing this she was killed last night. I only managed to make it to Timmy just in time."

"Thank God we only had one child, I don't think I could've protected more than one, not last night. Okay then, get him to me, he needs a mom and I'm gonna be the closest thing he's got."

"I'll get him to you but you tell the other girls to go slowly and cautiously and treat everyone that isn't with them in the house when the phone rings as a potential threat. Tell them all it's go time and to unlock the bag under the bed."

All of Buck's wives had an emergency bag prepared by him in case of something going wrong in Easterland; nothing had presented as a threat before, however there were always circumstances for which they had to be prepared. In the bags were passports kept up-to-date, specially sealed by the intelligence agencies throughout the world that were friendly to Easterland, a small medical kit, a large amount of cash and a loaded pistol with a silencer already attached. The girls all knew how to shoot and Buck was pretty confident they would be able to get the kids to Betty's house.

"Honey?" Betty said

"Yes?"

"I love you. Be safe, we all love you and need you to be safe. Get Timmy here as fast as you can then look after the rest."

"Love you too. See you soon."

FOREST FIRE

lames were spreading throughout the neighbourhood now. It was surprising just how many people had electrical things on or were cooking when the attacks took place. Palls of smoke hovered above Easterland, like one of those wraith things in that movie about a boy wizard waiting to take them all the way to prison, the sky was getting darker. No thanks to the force-field now, trapping them in. Buck had to get to headquarters but first needed to make sure the kids were safe. As much as he hated to admit it, they were the future of Easterland and the program and everything else that they worked so hard in years gone by. He had, to be honest, lost count. He just hoped all the other parents were able to take the same sort of precautions and get the kids. Buck had a bad feeling that wouldn't be the case.

Zombies? Here in Easterland. Question and statement, the two mixed together This was a New World Order, and it wasn't a period of time where the rabbit had to even pause. Think about it, the zombies were real. We all knew that, he just didn't think they could get in here. He just didn't think anyone would've ever put them in here for something as simple as chocolate, not something as simple to disrupt the human experience of Easter. It really didn't matter what you believed in out there. Personally Buck didn't know what was there, and didn't pretend to. He knew that chocolate didn't mean the resurrection of the son of a God, it's just nice to eat. It made people feel good and maybe that was the problem. Maybe someone didn't want other people to feel good. He had been there on the day a certain stone had been rolled aside to reveal an empty tomb, but about that he would never say anything more at least not on this earth. That was a long time ago.

He liked the name, Buck. It was simple and easy to say. It was not his real name. Not the name given to him by his parents or God. In fact it was a name he had gone by for scant more than one hundred years.

Science says that chocolate makes you feel good. That it releases a chemical inside your brain when you eat it. If that's true, what they don't know is that Buck deliberately found and located it so that people would have a nice experience every time they ate some. The product even had a name… Happyness™.

TIME TO GO

Timmy grabbed supplies and was ready. He was a good kid. Buck checked his bag to make sure he hadn't put anything too ridiculous in there. Nope the kid had done a good job, pretty much. The only extra thing he popped in there was a hand-held gaming machine and even the charger. Fresh underwear and clothing made up the rest of it along with the big toothbrush his mother had bought him once his baby rabbit teeth had fallen out. That toothbrush was symbolic. They both knew that. Buck didn't let it slip, how the kid wanted to remember his mother with a toothbrush. So be it.

"Alright son, I've gotta go out into it but you've gotta come with me first. Let's just quickly see if we can get any Intel. I can't raise the base, that doesn't mean anything bad happened. It means I just can't get through."

They went downstairs and into the lounge room. Timmy made sure his bag was actually filled with the stuff he needed and then impulsively grabbed a couple of photos from the mantle. Buck made sure that the bloody mess on the carpet in the Hall which used to be his wife was covered over with the whole runner rug, but

Lucy's blood was starting to seep through and the whole downstairs area smelt of fear and fright.

Buck picked up the remote control and switched on the television, waiting for the streaming services to kick in. What felt like an eternity later resulted in one of the well-known newsreaders in Easterland being broadcast on every available service.

"And we are back right now to warn you about the current state of emergency in Easterland. Our residents are to remain inside, do not leave for any reason whatsoever. It appears that… Zombies are attacking from the human world. Our sources indicate it may have been a deliberate act of terrorism by the humans, but that is yet to be proven. Areas of downtown are now inaccessible and authorities are doing their best to keep the undead at bay."

Helicopters in the sky hovered over badly affected areas of Easterland. The place looked like a fucking warzone.

Special sniper forces brought in by Buck himself were on board. Tigers, lions, and bears. Oh my! He couldn't help himself. He just finished it like that every time. He had read Tin Man and that thought jumped into his head. They were all crack shots however he knew those guys didn't stand a chance of stopping what was coming. The infection rate was just too quick.

The Easterland police force were setting up barriers across two of the major highways. Little good that was going to do, as long as these things remained. The only upside was that the newly dead seemed to be moving at a more shambling space. They may have a chance…

The news reporter kept talking. He got caught up in what he was saying, visually, but the next line hastened Buck to action.

"On the lips of everyone in Easterland, both animals and humans alike. Is just one question, where is the Easter Bunny? Has anyone seen Buck?"

A picture of him appeared on the screen. Buck flicked the TV off. He knew what he looked like. He also knew it was time to go.

"Timmy?" He called out to his boy as he switched off the television. There was no point in making noise and attracting the zombies to the house in hopes of a meal that wouldn't be there. He wouldn't have time to bury Lucy and didn't want them tearing her apart,

"It's time to go, we're going to Auntie Betty's."

Buck furtively ducked his head out of the front door. It was still swinging off its broken hinges. Outside he could hear groaning and the sounds of aimless feet shuffling in the street. He looked at his pistol. He had reloaded it and put spare clips in his belt. It was going to be too noisy. He raised his finger to Timmy and went into the garage, unlocking the gun locker with the combination only he had. Buck pulled out a crossbow and the remaining bolts he had left. He counted about 20. Re-reuse and Recycle Buck thought to himself. This was not gonna be a fun experience for his son. He loaded the first round. Together, they tip-toed along the hedge and made their way out of the yard.

"We've gotta get out of this place. If it's the last thing we ever do."

RIGHT HERE RIGHT NOW!

Betty Bunny quickly hugged another one of the wives, and showed her and the kids inside the house. Buck's wives were a tight knit group, and all considered each other family. They all considered each other to be sisters and to be honest each other's children were their own. Buck was a good father, a good partner and a great provider. It didn't hurt that he was also the Easter Bunny. Inside the tidy lounge room there were about 15 kids with their moms. The smell of comforting carrot stew filled the small house.

Little hands held cups of soup, shaking as they tried to take a sip. She had spiked their drinks with just a pinch of herbs to calm them down and it was working. Not enough to fuck them up. She would never do that, but enough that they could sit there. Younger rabbits had massive energy as it was, and nervous energy could kill them. They all understood the importance of silence. Even the little ones thank goodness. Most of the kids were teens. She was partly convinced that Buck had gone and been snipped.

He swore he hadn't, but he always did it with a smile. She was glad that she'd been able to get onto him on the phone. There was a low thrum of power that made the house feel like it was gently vibrating. The Rabbit Hole™, powering up down in the basement used a huge amount of energy, and frankly, she was pretty sure that it didn't derive its power source from the outside power lines. A couple of times the portal had been clear, and she could see the interior of another room with technicians waiting. Once she tried to reach in, they immediately held up their hands telling her to stop. She couldn't hear them and didn't even think about what would've happened if she tried to pop through. Buck had told her never to use the Rabbit Hole™, it was dangerous and only for emergencies. She didn't open that Pandora's box until told to.

The indicators on the side of the Rabbit Hole™ were slowly lighting up green. She needed to get a move on. It was almost time.

She motioned to one of the other mothers and the rabbits turned around and started gathering the children and glanced through the portal. The technician that she could see clearly looked up at her. He was wearing a brightly coloured Hawaiian shirt and a pair of jeans. Even indoors he had on sunglasses, he lowered them and put them in his pocket, revealing an expressive grey face with massive eyes. Clearly not human. He lowered the clipboard and spoke the words clearly.

"Mrs Bunny? I'm Mike the Alien and we're about to activate the Rabbit Hole™ and get you all through. Welcome to the North Pole."

WHISPERS OF DARKNESS

t wasn't only the animals of Easterland that were monitoring the news there. There were also government agencies around the world with links to Buck's operations who also watched the President lounging back in his chair and looking at his commander-in-chief.

"Was this us? Did we fuck it up somehow?"

"No, sir, nothing to do with us",

"Now that's a different question altogether, so we still haven't been able to figure out the technology of Easterland, and the big bunny ain't talking about it. If it was a land with borders, it would make sense but that delivery highway simply materialises where it's needed and the trucks come out. We know he's friendly and he has helped us on more than one occasion. Some of the advancements we have made with medicine are a direct result of his intervention."

"So who then?"

"Hard to say, but there is still that rumour that whoever created this problem in the first place, wherever they are, might have a hand in it all. It's like triage so we're just treating it case by case.

"Okay, hard to prepare for something that you've got no idea how to help with, but make sure that bunny has all the resources he might require. I know he likes guns, big guns."

The President leaned on the table, tapping his lips with his hands.

"For fuck's sake. I should've thought of this ages ago, you were saying there were still holes left in the shield? Just not big enough for us to get vehicles through?"

The Chief looked. "Yes, they are closing rapidly though."

"Then we need to move rapidly."

The President stood up decisively, "Where has the highway materialized?"

"At the moment, in Southern California."

"That might just work," the President said.

"Notify Naval Base San Diego: tell them on my executive power to fill three, no fuck it four gun lockers with things that go bang and boom. We may not be able to get boots on the ground there but we can make sure the Easter Bunny has as many weapons as possible. He's gonna need them. Set up a mobile command station near the highway. I will be personally spearheading this operation.

The Chief looked surprised, "But sir?"

"Don't but sir me, this is the motherfucking Easter Bunny, it's bad enough that most of the world doesn't believe he even exists. I'm not gonna lose him to a bunch of fucking zombies or whoever the fuck is controlling them. Get cracking."

"Yes, sir."

The Chief sprinted from the room, and the President sat back down and impulsively picked up the radio.

"And Chief?"

"Yes sir?"

"Put a couple of radios in there, just in case we can get through. That bunny may need Intel that only we can provide or worst case we may need the Intel that only he can provide just in case things go… carrot shaped."

RUN THROUGH THE SUBURBS

The scenes in Easterland were playing out like some bat shit animal documentary in the human world. Fleeing residents were being overwhelmed by the forces of evil as the undead attacked without discrimination on anything living. Hidden in the bushes, Timmy watched with horror as a family of deer ran down the street dressed in what appeared to be only their pajamas. Timmy started to call out to them but stopped. The amount of undead following was just too many.

"Run, run, run", the big male panted. The entire family had dropped on all fours, a sight generally unseen in Easterland now. But the increasing speed did very little to help save them. At the end of the cul-de-sac another horde appeared. It would've been ridiculous under normal circumstances. A tribe of squirrels stood at the other end. Slowly, making their way out of the trees blocking the way, the deer kids ahead of the parents skidded along the asphalt, their hooves knocking up pieces of tar as they tried to put on the brakes before hitting the little creatures in the road.

"For fuck's sake, keep going," Buck said. Timmy looked at him.

"They don't want to hit the squirrels, Dad."

"Look closely, son. They're not fucking squirrels any more. Keep going, keep going."

But it was too late. The parents caught up with the children and the four deer moved about in circles as the undead animals mixed in with a couple of undead humans. *How many of these fucking humans have got through?* Buck thought to himself. The big male deer closed in with his powerful hooves, striking out. It pushed them back for a brief moment, looking as though he may have cleared a path, but then from the treetops more squirrels dropped. All covered in blood and gore from their own, and the blood of others. A squirrel dropped onto the head of the male deer, holding onto its ears and scraped its teeth hard over the head of the deer, pulling the skull backwards. The teeth on bone sound was horrible and made Buck's balls retract.

The zombie squirrel didn't react as its big front teeth broke off into the head of the deer and the big mammal screamed with pain. The rest of the animals were swarmed as their clothes were torn from their bodies, the undead, seeking out the tender soft flesh beneath. The scene of the attack was a bloody gore filled frenzy, and as his own family got destroyed in front of him, the big male deer started turning, having been affected by the saliva from the squirrel. First he weaved about striking and trying to take down as many of his attackers as he could, until finally he succumbed, turning into the undead, whilst still on his feet. There was a sudden twanging sound, and a blue bolt smashed directly into his head. The male deer stood for maybe two seconds, and slammed into the ground brain-dead. The entire family was dead and other than a couple of furtive tears of flesh, the zombies were no longer interested in this meal. Like a weird, moaning mist they dispersed throughout the neighbourhood, disappearing back into the shadows and cover of trees, looking for more food.

Buck lowered his crossbow, he couldn't do that all day. They needed a better solution. They were losing time going so slowly, but he was pretty sure it was the one thing that was keeping them both alive. Once they were certain the undead were gone, they crept down to retrieve the bolt. It felt a little bit stupid but he had no idea how many times he would need the fucking thing. He braced his foot against the head of the deer and with a splintering noise the bolt came loose off its skull sending a light splatter of brain juice across his feet.

"Fucking gross!" Timmy said.

"You got that right kid."

Buck wiped the bolt clean on the deers clothing and put it back into his quiver whilst getting back on his feet. He looked about and it seemed clear, but the noises in the distance were horrific. He hoped Betty had sorted out the Rabbit Hole™.

In the meantime they had problems of their own. The Hillside Mall loomed in the distance with cars parked outside and a visible swarm surrounding it. They had to go through there in order to get to Betty's. The Mall? Buck fucking hated shopping.

He also hated murdering his neighbors.

INBOUND AND DANGEROUS

Accessing the World Wide Web, cameras were sending the footage back of the carnage in Easterland along an acute data route known only to a couple of people on the dark web. Things were progressing as planned, but that forcefield was not going to lower in time. Well it didn't appear that it would. It hadn't been made clear why they were told to shove a few zombies through into this part of the world. In a darkened van an operative for the Federal Government was positive that there was a good reason for it, but it was way above his pay grade. And way to dangerous to ask why of his other employer. The same entity that employed the March Hare.

What he hadn't expected though, was just how easily the infection spread from human to animal. When he was first told about the assignment, there was no way he would've expected to actually find a secret magical land filled with walking talking animals, wearing clothes and living normal lives. Well, actually is it normal? They were living like that? Still hasn't been determined exactly where the hell this land was. There was no landmass that matched up to it, and reports had been that it just simply appeared as required in multiple countries.

The few encounters that people had generally matched up and were the same, though for some reason during those encounters, they all said that the animals were speaking their language, not in a sign language kind of way, quite literally in the language of the area the landmass appeared in.

He wished he could get into Easterland and get to work with some of his tools. The boss said after this was done, there was a chance that could happen, he smiled and pushed the button that opened several small cages, just on the outskirts of the magical highway that had appeared in San Diego. The sides dropped and little shapes swarmed through the defensive barrier enclosing East-erland. The sound of a group of helicopters broke him out of his daydreaming and he went outside.

On the other side of the highway, Air Force One touched down on the ground with a thud. The President got out and hurried into one of the tents that had been set up. No media had been invited to this landing, though they were certainly there; that many cop cars and army vehicles setting up a small camp in suburbia tended to do that.

"People," the President was all business. "We up and running?"

One of the military leaders straightened up and saluted, "Yes, sir. We've managed to set up this space as you can see-"

"Yes yes yes, spare me the obvious details."

"Okay well, we have prepared the weaponry that you suggested, great choices by the way, and we have them ready for insertion. The idea is that we're gonna place an echo locator on each container. Hopefully that will get the attention of... Well, whoever it is that you want picking them up, sir. From there, we should be able to monitor, in a sense, the location of the containers should your agent move them."

"I just hope you find them in the first place," the President said,

"This is a hell of a gamble, but Easterland is on the line and more importantly, the fate of the free world may lay within those containers. Get cracking."

The President sat down at the head of the table, and monitored the action through the screens that had been placed there. Men and women bustled about adjusting things and moving things around. He had no idea what they were doing half the time. Sometimes he was under the impression that they were simply moving around quickly to make him think that they were busy, doing a lot of things that could've been done with simple button pushes. It was hard to bite his lip and say nothing when he just wanted to say hurry the fuck up. Eventually, however, footage of the weapons and munitions containers appeared on the screen and bomb disposal robots were ready to push them through the shimmering forcefield.

"We are ready, sir, when you are."

"Just get them through," he said, gesturing with his finger.

"Weapon push in 3...2...1", the technician said through the headset and the bomb disposable disposal teams moved forward, the remotes held in the hands. Slowly, the heavy weapon cages pierced through the forcefield of Easterland, a vibrating sound filled the air, and even at this distance, the President could hear metal rattling within metal as objects of this earth transitioned to something that could be utilized on that other dimension, that was his own theory at any rate. He wasn't a stupid man, but he knew that he still didn't belong here, at least not in the traditional sense. Other forces were at play, and after the events several years ago at the North Pole, this was a whole new world order and his finger was in a lot of secret pies.

Eventually, the last of the weapons were pushed through, and with a shimmer and a popping noise, the forcefield collapsed and closed.

"Translocator is working. However jammers are stopping us from mapping the area," one of the technicians announced to the leadership team. Best we can do is use the echo locators to give us a spatial awareness of the area, just how big it is etc, but it seems to be in flux constantly. All we really know is whether things are moving or not And the code is set to your specifications."

"Thank God, hopefully it gives that bunny a chance."

SHOPPING TRIP

"Is that the mall?"

"Dad? Are you sure that we have to go there? I hate that mall!" Timmy turned sulky. Buck didn't blame him. This sneak approach was allowing them progress, but it was a lot slower than what he would've hoped for. He wasn't really set up for an attack of the scale or this kind to be honest. If they got through this, a lot of changes would need to be made. He checked his radio again. There was no connection but hopefully there would be higher up in one of the levels of the mall. There was a carpark at the top, maybe if they got up there, he'd be able to get a direct line to HQ. The sound of flesh being ripped and bones being broken filled the air from the direction of the carpark directly outside the shopping centre.

The area was filled with the undead and the carloads of animals that had thought it might be a good idea to all rush to the same place at the same time to get survival gear. Personally, Buck would've gone to the hardware store down the road, but he was sure it would be like this as well. This place was filled with your normal things not survival quality weaponry.

A small sparrow, dressed in leisure wear stumbled on the high-way, having forgotten its ability to fly, unseen, unnoticed. A pig's trotter slammed down hard, pulverising it into the earth. It didn't even have time to cheep. The scent of blood drew fifteen animals to the mess on the road, where once they discovered there was nothing living, turned around and continued their silent patrol of the car park out the front of the mall.

Buck thought, hard. Maybe, just maybe there was a distraction to be made here after all. He felt terrible, and the idea was horrible, but there were just too many of them to take on. Buck got Timmy to turn around and kneel down and started rifling through the kid's backpack still strapped to his shoulders.

The teenage rabbit asked, "Dad, what are you doing?"

"Did you bring your slingshot?" asked the Easter Bunny.

"Yes."

"Don't think poorly of me, but we're going to make a mess."

Splat! The body of the Wren made a wet pelting sound as it hit the car and the animals, turned and shambled toward it. Timmy grabbed more crawling zombie birds from the ground and handed them to his dad, being careful to not put his paws near their tiny beaks. He felt utterly terrible. Was this bullying? He had no idea but these bird zombies were so stupid! His dad gathered them up and loaded them into the slingshot before sending them on their last flights.

He was not a bully at all. He actually had friends at school who were birds. Good friends but not dead friends. This was something altogether unexpected. The bigger animals still seemed to possess a horrible undead cunning of a sort, as though the infection had its own instinct. The birds nada zip zilch. Brain dead zombie birds!

He had to hold a paw up to his mouth to stop the laughter, feeling terrible. He looked at his dad and saw exactly the same expression on the Easter Bunny's face.

"What? Don't look at me like that," but he giggled. This wasn't the time or place for laughter.

"Watch this," he said and shot a pigeon into a straight road sign. His aim was amazing, and the bird splattered. The zombies whirled about again, confused by all the noise and the smell of blood.

A zombie cow lurched about drunkenly, striking its head against a street sign as its tongue tried to reach the blood, dripping just above. It smeared across its face, exposing skull as it tore itself apart, trying to reach the remains of the pigeon. Other animals gathered about, mouths open, eyes vacant. *It just might be enough,* Buck thought to himself.

In the distance, maybe about 30 feet away, a tiny movement caught his eye. A small family of cats were stuck in a car. With the number of dead here, it was a miracle that they had not been torn out of their vehicle.

Unless the dead can't figure out how to open doors, Buck thought to himself. That was a possibility. He had seen them ignore open doorways in the human world. Things that are obvious to the living just didn't seem to register to them. The cats were terrified and understandably so. The two little ones in the back, and they were young kittens, were trying to keep as still as possible, whilst he could see the mother turning back in her seat, trying to calm them down. The whole family would freeze every time a zombie approached, avoiding making eye contact. The car was covered with gore, clothing and fur splattered all over it. It could've been the gore that kept the others away. Maybe the car smelt like one of them? It would only be a matter of time before they screwed up though and became these monsters.

Became these monsters' dinner?

Buck and Timmy crept along the side of a few cars. Timmy reached out at one point, and pulled his dad's ears backwards as they stuck out well and truly over the bonnet of a vehicle, waving around like furry fingers, beckoning. Buck nodded in gratitude and peaked around the front grill of an old sedan in direct line of sight of the cat driver. He raised a paw up to his mouth as the cat saw him, the universal gesture for *be quiet*. Nearby, five zombies staggered and bumped their way about. Buck held up his paw in a Stop! gesture, then turned about, and let fly with another bird from the slingshot. The winged zombie tried to peck his paw as it left the slingshot and smashed into the side of a van. The thump moved the animals away from where the cats could exit the car and after an anxious fifteen seconds or so, Buck slid by the car and gently opened the doors.

"Be quiet," he said.

"Don't speak, just follow me."

"Mr Easter Bunny?" Said one of the kittens, a plump little fellow who needed help with his restraining belt tethering him to his car seat.

"Is that really you?"

"Yes, son, you need to be quiet. Can you do that for Mr Easter Bunny?"

The kid nodded and dropped from the seat to the ground outside silently as the rest of the family piled out. The mother reached to grab her purse, but the coins in it jangled, and stopped.

"Just leave it here. Money doesn't kind of matter at the moment". She nodded, and they crept back to Timmy waiting by the car.

From there, it was a short trip back to the mall itself. The zombies had all been agitated by the various small birds slamming into things, and for the most part, had moved away from an exit point generally used by the staff at the food court to take their rubbish bins out to the main dumpster. A couple of lanky hares remained, dressed as janitors and still holding their brooms as they fumbled about and twitched and convulsed on occasion.

There had almost been an Easter Hare instead of a bunny. That was actually a very close one, Buck thought. It would have changed his life and of course made it all that much shorter. It had certainly come down to the wire, Buck thought. A very, very long time ago.

He'd never really gotten along with Hares, but he respected

them. But these ones, they were a problem. In fact, there were a number of animals that might pose a problem, albeit of a different nature. He looked down at a small chicken pecking about aimlessly at the eye of one of the dead. Goop and stringy eye stuff was being sucked into its small mouth as it plucked and swallowed.

They had not been able to figure out why, but if animals came in from outside of Easterland, and it did happen, sometimes the magic or science that affected the rest of them didn't apply, and they would stay animals of a normal sort, becoming pets to other animals in order to make sure they stay safe. There were a lot more of them around than what he thought there was. But then his eye spotted movement to the side, a zombie chicken! He reached down, grabbed it, avoiding its horrid little beak and threw it as hard as he could.

BATTER UP!

The other janitor instinctively swung out with his mop broomstick, snapping it across the jaw of the other. The first hare was ripping its own face apart to get the blood off, and the other joined it, tumbling to the ground in a bizarre, rending mass of fur, ears and teeth. It took a few moments for the biting to stop once they realized there was nothing living there. It bought Buck all the time he needed to quickly usher the cats and his son inside and secure the access door behind him.

Betty's house waited just on the other side. He'd be able to get Timmy out of here and sort out this fucking mess. It was a very quick trip through the small shopping Plaza, literally from one side to the other. He slid the glass door open and looked about in the immediate vicinity. The car park ahead was utterly deserted, the undead, having moved away in a herd, attracted by the noise created with the birds on the other side.

The cats, a nice family by the looks of things, decided to stay inside the mall. They locked the door behind him and Timmy, and he hoped they weren't locking themselves in with the dead. He could see Betty's house just over the fence line at the end of the car park. Not long to go now.

THE RABBIT HOLE™

The Rabbit Hole™ felt uncomfortably warm. Betty Bunny stood next to it on the other side of the portal. A team had gathered to receive anyone she sent through. Upstairs, Buck's wives, and their children waited patiently. They were all good people and Betty was proud to be one of them. The other rabbits had come as quickly as they could once she had called them, making their way through the Warren and underground series of tunnels connecting the families of the Easter Bunny. It was a complex structure that Buck had made himself in secret. It wasn't for the sake of vanity that he had done so; Buck had tried to explain it, but Betty didn't understand. Not that she was a silly lady by any stretch of the imagination, but there was weird and wonderful magic holding the very fabric of Easterland together, and it all centred on there being an Easter Bunny.

The long story short was Easterland without an Easter Bunny would have wiped them all out and fast. Buck had to be there for their very existence to continue.

The indicator on the Rabbit Hole™ cycled itself to green, and she could see a similar light flashing green at the other end. It was hard to think of it as a tunnel of any sort, it looked as though they were stepping through a mirror into another world, and in a way they were. Mike the Alien had gotten her to pass several small items through earlier, and he had passed them back with no interference. She was amazed that no one had tried to get into the house yet. But, most of the folks around here would've had their own problems, or at least been hiding somewhere safe she hoped. There was a sudden sound from above, so loud she heard it even down in the basement. A shotgun. It was so loud that even the folk in the North Pole looked up.

"Betty?" Mike the Alien spoke up. "You need to go and sort that shit immediately. We cannot have zombies back in the North Pole again."

"Of course." Her paw closed over the small pistol she normally carried, but she did not draw it. No point in freaking out the other rabbits just yet. She made her way past the row of silent children on the stairs, and went to the living room. She felt like she was living in a cartoon. A grim parody sure, but a cartoon nonetheless. As though her life was… less.

However, this was the real world and what was happening outside, was enough to chill her to her very core.

In the front yard, running as fast as she could, Maureen, the last of the wives, fired back over her shoulder, ejecting shells as she desperately tried to put more in from the satchel around her waist. Behind her, moving at a surprising pace, five, yes, five raccoons stood at about 6 feet tall each. The big ones, Betty thought. They crashed through the undergrowth, all approaching the house. Ahead of her, Maureen ushered children, sweet little kids, raced ahead, screaming and panicking. They must've had their access cut off to the Warren to risk coming overland like this.

Betty pulled the door open and got the kids inside.

"Downstairs. Now," she said, no room for argument in her voice. The kids stumbled down the steps being helped by the other mothers.

"Get everyone through the Rabbit Hole™. Now." She yelled and pulled a pistol.

"You don't have to tell me twice," Mike the Alien said through the Rabbit Hole™. The portal was humming with an urgency as the gateway between Easterland and the North Pole was established. The gray alien was ready at his end to help the Bunny family over. If Buck was to fall, it would be one of these children who would have to pick up the mantel of Easter Bunny.

"Come on kids", Betty was aware the sounds behind her were upsetting the kids. The noise actually made the house vibrate within its very core; rattling at the stairs as though something was gonna explode behind her. She had to help Maureen now that all this extra noise was going to bring every single zombie in the neighbourhood to the house. There was no winning. Where the hell was Buck? Where was Timmy?

She got off a number of rounds and struck one of the raccoons in the eye. There was no reaction to the injury, but it did start blindly swiping about with its claws, snapping and biting.

The Rabbit Hole™ crackled as the kids slowly made their way through one at a time. A smell came up the staircase into the house itself. At first, she thought they were being fried as they went through, but it was just the discharge of ozone from the electricity being used to propel things through.

Maureen got to the door and spun around, dropping to her knee. Buckshot, no pun intended, blew forth from her shotgun, putting a hole in the chest of one of their pursuers. The zombies moved with an erratic, jerking motion as pellets filled their bodies.

"Head shots! Head shots!" Betty yelled directing the fire upward. Maureen blasted again, catching the raccoons in the face, her concentration pulling her mouth back in a fierce smile, exposing her long teeth. The force of the shotgun, made her ears flop about almost comically. She at least had the thought to tie them back with a headband. The shots polka dotted the raccoons, smashing in their teeth and exposing the inner workings of their heads, but they kept on coming. Most of the kids were through the Rabbit Hole™ now and a couple of the mothers anxiously awaited their children's turn.

With a crash, the bushes parted, and a huge brown mass sped into the front yard, immediately attracting the attention of the raccoons. It was Betty's neighbour, a huge elk by the name of Red, who reared and lashed out with his front legs crashing into the zombies in the front yard. The force of his blows stomping them to the ground, unable to get up.

"You get the fuck out of here. Get those kids to safety!"

He really didn't stand a chance. However, he did manage to buy them the time they needed to get the front door shut. Downstairs, the thump of energy continued as the kids went through. From each pulse, Betty figured there must've been a reset time for the Rabbit Hole™ to get back to enough power to accept the next person coming through. Thump! Thump! Thump! The last kid in the line was starting to make their way down the stairs, a few still in front of them.

Outside Red was struggling under the assault of the raccoons. Betty whispered a silent prayer as she watched his body covered by biting, sharp teeth. From what she had seen, it would only be a short matter of time before he was up and running and no longer on her side. They had to get the fuck out of there and fast. She looked at Maureen, her skin pale under her soft fur as she softly said, "Red…"

"That poor bastard."

" You know that we were dating? Maureen said. Betty looked at her shocked.

"You mean you and Red?"

"Yes, Buck knew about it. We were going to tell the rest of you, but we haven't been together for quite a long time. It doesn't mean I don't love the guy but I don't play with others you know that. I thought I could but… well I can't. I love you all, you're my family but I just couldn't share so I called it off. Some time later I met Red."

Betty looked at her. It made sense. Maureen was the youngest of the wives, and she and Buck did not have any children. Everyone just assumed it would happen. Maybe… Maybe she couldn't have any at this point, it really didn't matter. The only priority now was getting the kids and the rest of the ladies through that Rabbit Hole™ to the North Pole as fast as possible.

"Has Buck made it here yet? Maureen asked, but Betty shook her head.

"No he's meant to be here but he's probably gotten held up. Did you say there are fires over by the mall?"

"There's fire everywhere," Maureen said. "I think most of the forest is burning down right now."

A branch flicked through the air, embedded itself into the wall and hung there for a second quivering, then fell the ground.

"Fuck that was close come on. Let's get out of here."

The girls made it to the hall leading down to the basement. The wooden staircase was still filled with children, however, there were less of them now. They took their place at the end of the line and waited. Thump! Thump! Thump! Where the fuck are you Buck?

Timmy heard the sound of fighting first coming from Betty's home. He loved his aunt and the noise worried him. He looked back at his dad who was motioning at him to stop.

"Don't go jumping the fence. We don't know what's there. Give me a second and I'll scope it out."

He cautiously, peered over the fence into Betty's yard. A mass of bodies were on the front lawn, but he thought he recognised the next door neighbour, a nice guy by the name of Red being pinned down. He put away the crossbow. This was not the time for quiet.

"Okay son, we need to move quick. Do you remember how to use that pistol?"

"Of course I do, Dad!" Timmy pulled out the pistol from its small waist holster and slid back the action, safety off.

"Now," Buck said, "this is gonna be loud. It's gonna attract the attention of a lot of other things. God knows what."

Amongst the other undead outside the mall, Buck had noticed humans shambling around mixed amidst animals. They stood out like a sore thumb or a sore paw. It was clear they didn't belong in this land. There were humans here, but not many, especially because they had to be cleared by both human agencies and the special interest team at Easterland. These guys were not amongst that number and the odds of them finding a lamp by mistake… Nearly impossible.

Buck had a bad feeling that someone or something had deliberately brought the zombies in, he just hoped that he had the chance to find out who the fuck it was and jam a carrot up their ass. The air was thick with smoke. He could hear that the Rabbit Hole™ had been activated and breathed a sigh of relief. *Good girl Betty*, he thought, and together father and son came into view of the raccoons, just as Red staggered back up to his feet. His sweatsuit was ripped to shreds and covered in blood. His lips pulled back from his jawline, exposing busted and smashed teeth, making him look as though he'd been in a street fight.

Before he had fallen, he had managed to smash several of the raccoons to the point that whilst they were still able to move, it was with broken bones. But they still posed as much a threat as the undead elk.

Buck let off a shot. It hit a raccoon's centre mass and blood pooled out, but it did not stop the creature. A second round went through its eye, and dropped it to the ground. Behind the dead creature, Red lumbered towards Timmy with his hooves outstretched, and for some reason, all Buck could do was stare at the guy's wrist. That was his fucking watch! The one he kept at… Maureen's house. The timepiece jiggled about loosely on the narrow part of Red's foot. Looked as though Maureen had got over her heartbreak. They hadn't told the other bunnies, but he was going to go and see a lawyer about a divorce. The split had been amicable but it kind of made him feel butt hurt seeing his fucking watch on another man's wrist.

Timmy squeezed off a couple of shots. Two went wild and punched into the walls of the home.

"Careful kid," Buck cautioned. The young rabbit knelt, and held the pistol tightly with both paws, aiming down the centre as taught by his dad. He squeezed off another shot. It punched through the stupid watch and straight into the elk's head. The hard bones deflected the bullet, and the creature kept coming.

Fuck!

Buck launched into the air, propelling himself forward, and over the heads of the two zombie raccoons almost upon him. In a smooth motion as he landed in front of them, he stabbed one up and through the jaw with the knife, feeling it slide in through the software and the tip breaking, against the top layer of skull. It was enough though, and the raccoon collapsed onto him, scrabbling with its claws, as its nerve endings gave up the fight. The other one unperturbed by the death of its partner, opened its mouth to receive a bullet courtesy of Timmy. The back of its head exploded and brains flew and splattered against the face of the undead elk.

Buck rolled forward, grabbing a rake handle he'd spotted, snapping the stick as he went, creating a home-made spear. He thrusted upward, and it went through the chest of the raccoon, creating a flesh teepee as the creature was stuck. He grabbed its head and snapped it hard, feeling the neck vertebrae destroy under his paws. Whilst it didn't kill the raccoon, it did stop its motor functions, and it slowly slid down the broomhandle, leaving a bloody trail on the stick behind it. He placed the barrel of his pistol against its head and fired, and it stopped moving.

Meanwhile, Timmy was dealing with the elk. He'd only met Betty's neighbour a couple of times, and it looked as though he wasn't going to be invited in for coffee any time soon. He lashed out with his powerful legs knocking Red to the ground. The elk staggered back to its feet, slowly making its way back toward the living bunny, and that was when his dad hit the creature's skull with a rock. It was a cracking sound like a heavy duty egg being smashed with a hammer, the impact tearing flesh from bone and exposing the brain and blood ran down the side of the elks head and Buck hit again, hard, bashing grey matter which flew like a disgusting jelly all over the place. Brain destroyed, the elk went down.

It was so heavy that the ground thuddedwhen it hit. It was just a small vibration, but considering the fact, it was still amazing that there was a small shockwave. Buck was super glad he would never have to take that dude on, mano a mano. Kneeling down, he unclasped his watch from the dead elk and put it back on his wrist. That might be a conversation for later, but right now he better see how the kids are. He motioned to Timmy who ran ahead of his father and they went in through the door.

Thump! Thump! Thump!

Mike the Alien turned up the power output on his end of the Rabbit Hole™. At this rate the temporal Vortexx would not hold and they had to get them through as fast as possible. The ruckus that he heard through the portal up the stairs of the basement had subsided at least for now, but for all he knew the whole fucking town might've been coming in. He could see the line decreasing, in fact he thought the last of the kids had made it. The rest of the mothers were now in place at the North Pole, helping their young ones across the border one at a time.

Thump! Thump! Thump! At the end of the line, the last little rabbit ran back up the stairs as the basement door opened and slammed shut. Thank fuck for that, he thought as he saw Betty and another one of the rabbits wives come down the steps. *Homeboy doesn't fool around*, he laughed to himself.

He waved to Betty and made a gesture, and she sidled past the children, standing near the portal but not daring to look through it or go through it.

She said, "That's the last of them I don't think Buck's coming."

"What about his other kid?" Mike the Alien asked.

"He must be with his father."

"Okay then, we'll get you guys through. The Rabbit Hole™ was never designed to carry this many people. I can't guarantee it'll hold for much longer."

"Can we get them through a bit quicker? Maureen asked.

Mike the Alien blinked. "Let's try, but it's gonna make your room extremely hot." He glanced behind him, "Shields up", he said to the technicians. An energy field formed directly behind him. He moved all the children from the room and positioned himself.

"You weren't joking," Maureen said.

Mike the Alien looked sheepish. No fucking way come on. He made some adjustments to the console and the hammer power through The Rabbit Hole™ increased, it was hurting their ears. .

Thump! Thump! Thump! Finally, the last rabbit popped through, to the safety of the North Pole. The recovery teams got all the kids out, and Maureen looked at Betty. Betty said, "The kids need you. I'll be right behind."

Maureen didn't need to be told twice, teleporting through the Rabbit Hole™, turning around to see her friend. Her jaw dropping open and she looked behind Betty who then spun about pointing a pistol at the basement door, which flew open, showing two silhouettes.

Blam!

The gun jumped in her paws, just missing the two figures and tearing plaster from the wall. She lowered the pistol and readied herself for another shot.

"Hurry up," said Mike the Alien.

"There's only enough power for one more jump."

She could feel the power from the Rabbit Hole™, making her fur stand on end. She couldn't risk those two getting through to the children. They were coming down the steps now, and there was something oddly familiar about…

FAMILY

"Auntie Betty!" Timmy came into view and Betty dropped her gun in relief. If that was Timmy, behind him could only be Buck!

"Timmy" she stretched out her arms and the teenage rabbit ran into them, hugging her tight. In an instant, Buck was behind them, wrapping his arms around the two. For a brief moment, they stayed in that pose, until behind them on the other side of the planet or even another dimension, Buck wasn't sure how it worked, Mike the alien coughed politely, then yelled to break up the family reunion.

"Buck, the Rabbit Hole™ is collapsing."

Betty looked at Buck, who looked at Mike the Alien, who looked back at him and nodded. Buck looked at the read out on the edge of the portal. The device was at a dangerously low power, but both Betty and Timmy were small. He stood back from them, "Hold on tight to each other," he said.

"No Buck!"

"No Dad!"

"Yes to you both and don't forget I fucking love you."

Springing at them with supernatural speed and strength, Buck lunged into his family with the strength of a battering ram, feeling one of Timmy's ribs break under the impact. The two had the air knocked out of them as they flew through the portal together, still gripping onto each other tightly.

The energy that made the travel possible shimmered, sputtered, and failed, shrinking to the size of a dinner plate. The last thing he saw was the two of them, safe on the floor of the lab at the North Pole looking at him as the portal's power gave out and collapsed in on itself. Just before the power went out, he saw his wife mouth the words, 'Love you', then the Rabbit Hole™ died.

Standing in the darkened basement, the Easter Bunny reached into the ammo satchel at his waist.

The sound of the shells going into the magazine made a satisfying noise. He realised he was humming. What was the song... Mama said knock you out. Anyway, right now he knew his family was safe.

"It's time to fuck shit up," he said and left the basement. As he went up the steps, his phone started vibrating, making a very low, pinging noise. He removed it from his jeans and swiped the app open. It was a Geo locator set to a frequency that only he and a few others knew. Someone was making sure he found whatever the hell it was. And whatever it was, it better help him kill a lot of fucking zombies.

As he made his way toward whatever it was that had been left for him, Buck noticed that the streets were predominantly empty other than the undead. Every now, and then he would see a curtain move, which gave him hope. As long as people stayed quiet and didn't attract attention for the most part, they wouldn't be on the radar of the zombies who are naturally attracted to the living. Maybe, just maybe there was hope after all. His mind raced with a barrage of thoughts. Why had this happened? Who was behind it and what could he do to stop it?

None of it really mattered. All he needed to do was kick ass, both dead and alive.

TREASURE HUNT

The further Buck traveled through town, the more he could see people had been affected by the undead. Once bright eyes looked all scared. Furtive peeks outside were made behind curtains. On one occasion, a small child called out,

"Hey, Mr Easter Bunny." Buck turned around, startled by the noise. He was waiting for something, well anything to happen, but all it was was a fucking kid, a kid of all things, having the balls to look out from behind the door.

"Are you thirsty Mr Bunny?"

As quietly as he could, Buck made his way over to the child, a young ferret.

"I'm Bob!" said the ferret, handing him a glass filled with cold milk. Buck gulped it down feeling the Happyness™ in the chocolate fill him.

"Well kid, you know who I am?"

"Yes Sir, the chocolate milk… You better… Sir, have you seen my parents?"

Buck wiped the brown goodness from his mouth, and he realized that sounded all sorts of wrong, it wasn't that sort of book.

"Son, your parents… Well to be honest Bob, I think they're most likely dead." Just like that matter-of-fact. There was no reason to sugar coat it.

"Why do you think that? They went out because our neighbour's house was burning."

Buck glanced over at the neighbour's house. The charred remains of a building were there right next door. It was kind of fucking amazing that the flames hadn't jumped, but they hadn't and it was like that all over the place. Some buildings were burnt, others weren't. It was a fluke. He knew that the whole Easterland fire department had done the absolute crazy best.

"Are you gonna leave soon Mr Easter Bunny?" The ferret asked, breaking up Bucks reverie. Buck thought about it. In the meantime a neighbor had approached. Buck asked her name as she hugged Bob. Buck thought hard and fast.

"Trudy, take the kid. There's no fucking way he's safe here that's for sure." He had a look around in the kitchen. It was well stocked with food. In fact, it was overstocked. Maybe the kid's parents were doomsday preppers, or some shit like that. He wasn't entirely sure. Lucky kid.

"As much as I'd like to take you Bob, it's pretty dangerous out there at the moment. It's a lot safer with Aunt Trudy. You've seen all those things that are crawling around?"

"The zombies?"

"Yeah, the zombies. It's not gonna be safe out there and I can't guarantee that we won't get into the thick of it. As a matter of fact, I know that we will. It'll be far better for you to stay here. Lock the door behind me when I go and don't open it up to anyone, not even if they look like your parents. Not without talking to them first or hearing them speak more to the point. Don't make conversation, sound attracts them. Did you get that? Do you understand?"

"Got it", the kid said. "If it can't talk, I don't let it in." Buck reached out and tousled the ferret's fur and made cute noises. Buck gently let go of him, got up and straightened up his gear. He asked,

"Bob, do you know if Mom and Dad had any weapons hidden around the house?"

"I don't think so, Mr Easter Bunny. I think we only had the one gun and Dad took it with him when he left."

"Fair enough. Well, I better get going. Remember…"

"I know I know, lock the doors, don't open them unless someone can talk and even if they can talk, it's probably not safe. Don't make noise…"

"Good boy." Buck headed to the back door and opened it just a crack. He peeked out, but the backyard was totally empty of anything other than a couple of human shaped statues in the centre.

"I've got a couple of those at home too."

"I don't like them. I think they're creepy but Mom and Dad love them. Good luck Mr Easter Bunny." The kid shut the door quietly and Buck heard the chain bang and slide across, and then the door itself clicked shut.

Good luck kid, Buck thought to himself and kept on trucking.

MARCH HARE

The March Hare looked at his computers. For the most part, the holes in the forcefield surrounding Easterland were closed, trapping everyone inside, including him. He wasn't stupid, he realized that, however, he had no intention of going outside for quite some time. Now to figure out how this fucking thing teleported, and then how to deliver it to the client. Keeping the forcefield active was imperative, both to stop the resistance from within and keep interference from the outside at bay. The presence of the was going to be fairly shortly. The broadcast station he'd set up was helping maintain the pulse that reanimated the dead. If that went down, that would be the end of everything. The client had explained that the zombies weren't capable of teleporting with Easterland when the dimension shifted, so the forcefield needed to stay up until that was achieved. He had been scanning the news channels and so far, there had been no sightings of the Easter Bunny. That was both good and bad. He had really hoped that he wouldn't have to deal with the big bad rabbit.

He snickered and scratched his head. Outside his small hideaway in the security section of the mall, he saw a small group of cats moving about in the food court, looking about furtively as they scrounged for food. Never mind, they didn't propose any threat. Though for fun he might send the Armadillo Brothers at them and watch the action on the monitors.

He had to keep toggling the cameras between the interior and exterior views, and with all the excitement happening outside in the surrounding suburbs, had forgotten on more than one occasion to cycle through the different views available to him. Every now and then, he would switch over to the car park camera outside of the mall as another hapless idiot showed up only to be swarmed by the undead. They were always so hungry, he thought to himself. He didn't understand why they stopped eating once the victim was dead. He shook his head. Fuck that shit. He wasn't going outside until the job was done.

He panned through the cameras, pausing when he noticed, just inside the forcefield, two large black lockers that had not previously been there. They looked ridiculous in the middle of the field that they were in, but they were there nonetheless. He zoomed in and saw a small, blinking red light on each of them. How had they got there? He had to find out. He spun about in his chair and faced the brothers who stared at him expressionlessly.

"Do either of you know what those are?"

They both shrugged. Why would they know? They could only see what he could see, and the idiots had been fiddling with the cameras non-stop.

"Well we need to know what they are. I don't care which one of you, but one of you needs to go and find out right now."

"But boss that's right near the forcefield, wouldn't we be better off both staying here with you?"

"I think I'll decide what's best for everyone," the March Hare said, "No more discussion. I'm paying the bills. Go go go!"

The Armadillo Brothers looked at each other. Even though he was a dip shit and a crazy one at that, he wasn't asking for anything that was outside of the realms of their contract.

"Alright, are you ready?" The other one nodded.

"Rock, paper, scissors, 123?

Reggie looked at Max's hand, closed in a fist, impervious to his scissors.

"Um, best of three bro?"

"Not a fucking chance. It's about time I had a win."

"Okay, okay." Reggie slung his assault rifle over his shoulders. The strap cinched tight.

"Later boss."

"Make sure you take a radio numb nuts."

"How am I gonna find out what's in there?" Reggie said, He wasn't used to being spoken to like that by anyone other than his brother who had more than earned the right.

The March Hare ignored him or at least pretended to not hear.

"You watch me on a camera, wait till I come back. Motherfucker, you might be paying the bills, but you ain't got no right to be speaking to me like that. Do you understand?" Reggie took a step towards the March Hare who shrunk back into his chair.

"Okay, okay, I was just kidding. Go on, get out there."

"On my way." Reggie turned to his brother and gave him a hug. "Later, dick head." "Numbnuts," came the reply. The door opened, Reggie went out, shutting and locking it behind him. Max watched on the cameras as his brother made his way through the mall, entering through one of the non-public exit doors.

"He's on his way," he announced unnecessarily.

"I know, I know I'm watching him too," the March Hare said, cycling through the video feed in the mall.

"Leave that one on Reggie," Max said. "At least until he's outside, then I'll see if I can't throw some drones up. I may not be able to give him back up, but at least I'll know he's not alone."

March Hare left the camera on the lone Armadillo Brother, even going so far as to cycle to the next camera outside. Reggie, armed with a fighting knife and a machete, quickly dispatched the few remaining zombies in the entrance and then disappeared from view. Despite their immense size, the brothers were stealthy and a force to be reckoned with.

The Hare determined that it would take a good couple of hours on foot before Reggie reached the containers by the edge of the forcefield, which shimmered behind them obscuring his vision. He could just make out what looked like ten caravans positioned directly behind the containers, but on the wrong side of the shield.

Fucking humans he thought. What the fuck is in those things? He had a sneaking suspicion that someone was trying to provide aid to the Easter Bunny, which only meant one thing. Either the big guy was still alive, or at least someone thought he was and wanted to provide material aid which also meant another thing; whatever was in those containers was more than likely to be really useful.

He flicked the cameras over and settled back to watch as the undead hordes congregated to the east of the Hope Springs Eternal river. Right near the chocolate factory.

LOONEY TUNE

The pinging sound on Buck's phone was getting more insistent, the little device vibrating with each resonating sound. It was kind of hypnotic, and he could feel the adrenaline rush every time it kicked in. Then he realized, wait a second! No sound! No sound, and flicked his phone to silent, It still vibrated though let him know he was on the right track.

All of a sudden, the device became more insistent and Buck realised it was actually ringing. What the hell? He'd forgotten that people could actually talk to him on it. A Video call request came through, and he unmuted the phone and took it. As the screen coalesced into an image, he realised it was the head of his R&D at the chocolate factory, Doc Watkins.

"Ah what's up Doc?"

The human hated that line, and Buck insisted on doing it. Every time Doc Watkins called, he wished that he could set his phone number to private, but he knew that the Easter Bunny wouldn't pick up.

"Buck! We've been trying our best to get in contact with you for the longest time. Some of the guys even thought you were dead."

"Welp, not dead. I'm heading out to the edge of the forcefield. Someone's left something there for me, my locator is going off."

"Okay, well, we detected a surge of power at Betty's home, but I could not dispatch our operatives out there. By any chance did you activate the Rabbit Hole™?" The good doctor was one of the few people who knew about the existence of the Rabbit Hole™ for one simple reason; it was the only way of making sure that there was a contingency plan in place in the unlikely event of Buck biting the dust.

Buck nodded, "Yep sure did. Betty mentioned she got all the kids out to the North Pole before the damn thing powered down, but, at least they're all there, including Timmy." He took a deep breath and gulped, and then in a broken voice said, "I lost Mrs Bunny though."

The Doc looked down thinking to himself *which one?*, outwardly saying "Fuck, I'm really sorry Buck. I know what she meant to you."

"Someone's gonna fucking pay, I can tell you that right now Doc. One thing I do want to ask you is how the fuck did they get through the forcefield? I honestly thought we were dodging that shit!"

"It's not that the forcefield didn't work, it's simply that someone timed their incursion to come inside with one of our delivery trucks. It was as simple as following and making their way through when our vehicles pass through a deactivated part of the forcefield. There's a short amount of time before that area can be reactivated again. We don't want to go chopping our vehicles in half if you know what I mean. So basically someone very quickly drove a truck in directly after our delivery vehicle filled with those monsters. We've recently been able to clear up the video footage and, unfortunately Buck, that someone is someone that we know. I'm sending the video to you now."

Buck looked down at his phone. In a video streamed from one of Easterland's many security cameras, there by the perimeter, he could see the footage of one of the Easterland trucks coming back home to base. The shimmer of the forcefield powering down as an authorised truck passed through.

"Now you see how the truck went through," the professor said. "Keep watching. They managed to disable that camera, but not before we got a very quick glimpse at who was driving."

You had to watch really carefully to see the footage. Buck could see just behind the delivery truck, a smaller box shaped truck, almost directly behind it. In fact, it was so close they were nose to tail. The footage zoomed in and there was no mistaking it. The face of the March Hare appeared. Just before the camera died, Buck saw the March Hare give it the bird and then push a button on a small box and the video footage ended.

"That motherfucker," he said, scratching his whiskers. "It's the – –"

"March Hare," the Doc finished his sentence.

"But one of the things we're trying to still figure out is why would he have done this to Easterland?"

"That part's easy. He's bat shit crazy," said Buck having on more than one occasion to lock the Hare up Downtown. It was always for minor things. Idiot thought that he was a super villain, and that Buck was his arch nemesis. The Hare was a petty thief with delusions of grandeur, and did not have the wherewithal to pull off a job of this magnitude, but it looked as though he was the one who was pulling the strings, at least on this side of the forcefield, and he was the one that Buck would have to find at some point, he thought through gritted teeth.

It would be a lot more than just a simple talking to the March Hare. He would get it this time. Lots of good people were dead because of that idiot, including his own beloved wife.

He kept moving toward his objective; the containers with the homing devices on them just there in the distance. In the field, actually, it was a little bit too small to be called a field, it was a green area with a kids playground and a little bit more bushland just behind it. The containers stood out like sore thumbs. So did the zombies that were walking around nearby.

"I've gotta go. I'm almost at the containers. They look like some sort of big tool chests, that's just a guess, but there's a couple of undead directly behind the playground here that I'm gonna have to deal with first. At least they're humans, not any of us."

"Buck? You do know that I'm a human, too,' the Doc said.

"You don't count Doc," said Buck. "Whether you like it or not, you're part of Easterland now. You're one of us."

"Roger that. Good luck. I'll keep trying to pinpoint the March Hare's location. I'm genuinely interested in what's in those containers so if you have time please do keep me updated.

FIGHT MUSIC

"Okley dokely." Buck started to limber up, hopping up and down on the spot to get his adrenaline going. There were enough of these douche bags to keep him on his toes. He clicked off the phone, slipping it back into his pocket. Looking around, he saw there were five zombies. No, make that six. One had somehow climbed up to the top of the kids playground, and was at the top of the fort connected to a slide that circled a large pole. Another had its ankle caught in the chain of a swing, and two others were playing on a seesaw. The other couple were just rolling around, not taking advantage of the fun that the Easterland Council had provided. Stupid humans.

Buck took aim with his crossbow and let fly. The bolt flew true, piercing the head of the human at the top of the slide with a grunt. It fell backwards and slowly made its way down the plastic slide, the blood oozing from its wounds creating a lubricant to aid its progress. It was still painfully slow and Buck looked on in morbid fascination. It arrived motionless at the bottom, slipping off and onto the wood chips at the bottom.

One down, Buck thought. He put away the crossbow and

pulled out the machete tucked behind his back. He banged it hard against the bars of the fort, the sound of metal striking metal echoing. The zombies heard the noise and slowly and painfully fell off the equipment they were on and rising to their feet. The undead shambled toward him, hunger in their eyes. A song started playing inside Buck's head.

♫ Ahhh ahhh ahh ah ahhh ahhha hhh ahhh. Don't call it a comeback. I've been here for years keeping suckers and tears. I'm gonna rain down on you like a monsoon. Listen to the bass go boom! Explosion, overpowering! I'm gonna knock you out. Momma said, knock you out!♫

The smell from the undead was overwhelming. Buck thought that he was gonna puke, but he kept on going. What else could he do? He had to get to those containers by the end of the field, and the only way to do it was to go through it. The first zombie that used to be a lady with long blonde hair came toward him. The smell from her was a mix of vomit and department store perfume. One of her eyes had decided to leave her face and was hanging by its stalk. The other lolled around wildly and her tongue was stuck out from between her teeth as they jumped on its rubbery surface. She was wearing a house dress with a pretty flower pattern and for a moment Buck could've imagined that she would've been a pretty nice lady when she was alive.

"I'm sorry lady," he said and somersaulted along the grass, and as he sprung up, his powerful legs propelled him forward and swung toward her face, with an undercut that split her from the chin to the top of her head like a massive tree falling in a forest.

"Timber!"

Her head slowly cracked open from the face, revealing the broken jaw, teeth, nasal cavity and the rotting brain inside her head.

She said nothing and died, her manicured, broken nails scrabbling in the bark for a few seconds.

Buck felt fingers digging into his back. The pain was excruciating. The other numbskull had taken advantage of the fact that he spent too much time with the first lady and it had snuck up behind him. Well, not snuck, and that made it even worse. This thing, without any real brain, had managed to creep up behind him without creeping because he was a douchebag who wasn't paying attention. The pain jolted him, but fortunately, the zombie's fingers did not break his skin directly. They tore out chunks of fur from his back as it maintained a grip on his jacket. It still hurt, but he was grateful for the wake up call.

He spun about and the stupid thing still held onto him. His momentum made it fly through the air, as though he was an adult giving a child a whirlybird. He kept spinning until he realized he didn't have much time to be mucking around. The seesaw kids were now off the ride, and quickly making their way toward him.

Some part of the back of his brain was more than fully aware of how fucking stupid all this looked. Then again, to a lot of humans the idea of a six foot rabbit, dressed in human clothing fighting a zombie that was holding onto its back was both hilarious and ludicrous.

Buck spun around like a children's amusement park. Would've been damn hilarious if the outcome wasn't fatal. He increased the speed. Just as he was going as fast as he could. He reversed and spun back the other way, causing the zombie to let go of his back. Thank fuck for that he thought.

The undead spun through the air like a lazy frisbee and impaled its skull on one of the metal handles of the seesaw, making it slam to the ground as half of its brain pan was ripped up, pulping what was left of its cranium in the process. The zombie's body slumped down onto the seat, like a child that had fallen asleep after having run out of energy in the middle of playtime.

He heard a guttural roar and pulled out his hunting knife. The two smaller figures that had previously been on the seesaw were circling around the fort, their teeth gnashing in anticipation of chewing on his soft bunny flesh.

"What the fuck?" he said, and took a step back at the sight

before him. They were fucking kids, a little boy and girl, identical twins by the looks of things. He couldn't get over that stupid habit that some parents had of dressing their fucking children in the same clothing to therefore confuse them even more and their friends as to who the fuck was who. Except for the fact that half of their faces had been torn off, they were kinda cute.

"Naw, how adorable," he cried out loud, and sprung toward them. The closest one, the little girl noisily swung her arms out in a clawing motion to try to grab onto him.

"Not so fast cupcake," he said, pirouetting between them and shanking her in the temple as he did so. The blade stuck in her skull, and she followed his trajectory, quite like the zombie before her. Buck smashed her into her brother, who fell down underneath the little girl's body. Collateral shot for the win! Buck sprung backwards, releasing the knife as he went into a full on reverse somersault landing down on the hilt of the weapon, driving it through both of their heads.

The force was so extreme that the girl's head caved in under the finger guard of the knife, and the little boy was stomped into the bark, so deeply that only a small part of his head was visible. Buck really didn't want to see what it looked like underneath all that mess.

"Sorry kids, playtime's over," he said. Now there was one to go.

"Oh you have to be shitting me," he said out loud. It was an old lady, well, an old zombie lady in any case, making her way toward him with such painful speed as she struggled to maneuver her walker with her dead fingers. As she opened her jaws backwards and forwards, her dentures fell out, shattering on the metal bar she was holding onto. It reminded him of that made up story on that TV show where a lady with a sword drags around two zombies with their jaws ripped out.

Granny here had been rendered ineffectual by her sudden lack of teeth. Still, he thought to himself, no point in risking her messing anyone else up. The old lady zombie hobbled toward him, her face drawn back in a sneer. He picked up the walker, and she tumbled to the ground where he proceeded to cave her head in with the legs of the device as she struggled to get back up. Eventually, she fell still and Buck for a split second, felt kinda bad. For a split second. Then he shook his head, feeling his ears, swaying in the breeze and sprinted the remaining distance to the black containers.

The locator on his phone was going bat shit now, so he knew he was at the right place now. But with all seriousness he could actually see the boxes directly in front of him and no longer needed the locator running.

EL PRESIDENTE

The forcefield was shimmering directly behind the containers and he noticed movement and what appeared to be some tents.

"Buck!" Came a voice amplified by a bull horn. He saw the familiar features of the President coming toward the forcefield on the other side.

"I suggest you don't try to come through," Buck said. "Things are a little bit fucked up here at the moment."

"Yes, yes we know about that," the President said. "That's why we pushed these containers through just before the forcefield closed. Sorry we couldn't send troops. This is the best we could do considering the circumstances."

"That's fine," said Buck. "Any help is greatly appreciated. What have we got in there?"

"Well," said the President, "there are all sorts of goodies in there that should help you out. We're not sure of the situation there, but it looked pretty grim before the forcefield went down totally."

"Yes, it's pretty messed up," said Buck, "but I do have a beat on who caused it and trust me, they're gonna get what's coming to them."

"Good work," said the President. "Anyone we know on this side?"

"I fucking wish," said Buck. "But it's one of ours. He calls himself the March Hare but in all honesty, he's a sad little fuck. He is obviously being controlled by someone else from out in your world or a parallel dimension similar to yours. He's the one at the moment who's causing all these problems and who, I believe, invited all of our new party guests into Easterland."

"How much damage is there at the present?" The President leaned forward.

"Sir, it's a shit show. I knew you had problems with the Undead since the Pulse but…"

"Fucking zombies," said the President.

"Fucking zombies," said Buck.

IT'S BEGINNING TO FEEL A LOT LIKE EASTER

Buck placed his hands on his hips, "how do I get into the containers? He asked the President behind the forcefield.

"Oh that's easy, it's a combination," he said. "Simply enter in my birthday."

"What format?"

"US Buck, month month day day year year year year."

Buck stared at the numeric pad and the president looked on expectedly. "You're really gonna like what's in there Buck. I think it's everything you'll need."

"Hmm… I'm sure it will be. There's only a slight problem sir."

"Yes, what is it?"

"How the fuck am I meant to know when your birthday is? What a stupid passcode. I've got 23 children and I know barely all of their birthdates. Why would I know yours?"

The president looked sheepish.

"Yes, my advisors told me that this might prove to be a problem. Okay, well, its-" and he rattled a series of numbers that Buck punched into the combination lock which hissed open on pneumatic doors.

"Motherfucker," said Buck as he stared inside. Everything he would have wished for to wage a one man war on the undead was waiting for him. Pistols, ammunition, shotguns, machine guns, light machine gun, sub machine guns, grenades, grenade launchers, surface-to-air missiles… Just kidding about that one, that wouldn't fit, but last but not least up the top was something that made Buck's heart stop. He hadn't used one in a long time; an RPG.

"Mr President, you shouldn't have," he exclaimed in excitement and started loading up.

"It's the least I could do," the president said, a big smile on his face visible, even through the shimmering forcefield.

"After all, we do have a contract with the good people of Easterland,"

"Indeed you do," Buck said as he filled one of the empty backpacks in the containers with ammo and grenades.

"That aside, thank you so very much. All of this will help, though at the moment, the factory is in lockdown and is surrounded. At least that's what I've been told, and every time one of these fuckers gets a hold of one of my people, they become one of them. At the rate it's going, there won't be many people left to do deliveries."

"We have the same problem here," said the president. "In fact, we still do even though the numbers have dwindled down a little bit. But even so, I don't go anywhere without at least five agents for personal protection."

Buck checked out the containers. There was more than he could possibly carry, but depending on the amount of undead, he may simply have to come back here for more. He grabbed a series of throwing stars, some daggers, and a hatchet.

And bullets. A lot of bullets.

Fuck! he felt like he weighed a ton, but he planned on using a lot of that ammunition, and in pretty short order that would lessen the weight.

Buck turned and faced the president, "Alright, so it looks like

I've gotta get going now. Time is of the essence. I managed to get my wives and kids out of here"

"The Rabbit Hole™?" The president asked.

"Yeah, they are as safe and sound as they can be in the North Pole."

"Yes, I'd agree with you on that one. I've still got Nick and Carol stationed there. They're good agents. Your family will be safe there."

"I certainly hope so," said Buck. "I've still gotta figure out how to get back to them."

"Buck, you have a problem," said the President. "Behind you, now!"

AMBUSH! SORT OF!

Buck turned around quickly, his ears smacking against the side of his head as he did so. In the distance, he could see a large shape hurtling toward him on the other side of the playground. It was moving too quickly to be one of the zombies. He didn't know what it was, but it was fucking huge.

"Well Sir, it was so good to chat to you, but it looks like I've gotta take care of business here."

"Godspeed son," said the president and headed back behind the safety of the barriers that had been erected. He didn't know if the forcefield could stop whatever was coming and he didn't want to stay around to find out. For all he knew, they could've been coming for him. He WAS the president after fucking all.

Buck thought fast; there was no way he could get around this thing. It was moving so damn fast, almost as fast as he could move. The thing was, how was he going to go back through the playground in order to get back to the city and make his way to the chocolate factory? They were onto him.

You got this he told himself as he fidgeted. It was almost worse than seeing the undead coming towards him. He couldn't figure out what this thing was, because it was a little bit too far away, even for his keen sight, and considering the fact he was the Easter Bunny, there was no point in telling himself he should've eaten more carrots to improve his vision. It was already more than twenty-twenty.

He started toward the oncoming target, gradually increasing speed on his long legs. The adrenaline was starting to rush through him again. Whatever the hell it was, it was huge, at least as tall as him. Maybe a little bit taller, but the width of the thing... And that was when the bullets started whizzing past him. He could hear them smacking into the forcefield, melting as they hit it. It sounded like static electricity, sort of like when a fly goes into a trap and gets buzzed by the UV light.

Even with his heightened abilities, it was hard to duck and dodge around the oncoming bullets. One punched through the top of one of his ears. Buck felt a burning sensation and blood starting to trickle down into his ear canal. The hole started to close over, almost immediately, but it wasn't fast like in the movies. Yes, he had an unnatural or supernatural ability to heal, he was the fucking Easter Bunny after all. He would even go as far as to say that he was nearly, yes, nearly immortal. It sure as hell didn't mean that he was invulnerable.

In a way he was kind of like the undead all around him. A bad enough brain injury would mean permanent death; a big enough blow to the heart, same thing. Otherwise, most things grew back, including... Well, possibly this isn't the time or place to go into that.

From that moment on Buck had learned to be a lot more choosy about the people he slept with. And that was the other side of things too; he truly loved each and every one of his wives and children. He found it kind of funny that it was similar to the human world, and their normal rabbits. But you factor in the immortality and shit got different.

There was a process before he found a new wife that included the approval of the others. Over the centuries he found it simply meant there was overlap but it sure as fuck also meant that he had love enough for everyone.

It kind of saddened him that his wives gained a little bit of longevity from him but ultimately, they would fade and be returned to the Earth from which they came.

Anyway, he'd been shot in the ear, and it fucking hurt. The pain brought him back to the present though, and he snarled, his whiskers bristling!

"You motherfucker!"

Buck sprung forward, blasting the machine gun, spraying at the oncoming figure.

REGGIE!

eggie jumped up. He was pretty sure he had tagged whatever was ahead. He didn't give a shit what it was, it was in the way of the black containers that the boss wanted to find out more about. He'd watched from a distance, as this guy had taken out those zombies. Pretty neat footwork. He saw the machine gun swing up and didn't wait to see what would happen. He jumped into the air, curling into a ball, his armoured plating easily deflecting the bullets. He hit the ground with a thud and kept rolling. In this protective state, he couldn't use any of his weapons or get ready for the next assault, but he was damn near bullet-proof.

As he spun through the air, he felt the bullets ricochet off his hardened shell with his head, tucked deep into his stomach. The sound was muffled, kind of like when you've been to a rock concert, and then go outside, and try to talk to your friends. As long as he kept everything nice and tightly together, it would take a lot more than a pistol, or even a machine gun like this rabbit had. He could see now; it was a rabbit that was firing at him.

Almost no noise penetrated his armored shell. He felt a bullet glance off him as he hit the ground and continued to roll towards the target. He still had a strong grip on his pistol. He was ready to fire when he unrolled. And that's when the RPG hit him.

For fucks sake, I think that's one of the Armadillo Brothers, Buck thought to himself. He'd heard about them, shit, he had seen photos of them. He'd just never seen one in real life. He swept the machine gun up and let loose but the fucking thing curled up in mid air and all he heard was the ricochet of his bullets as they bounced off the thick scales of the armadillo.

It was happening in slow motion, the armadillo spinning, his clothes making a flapping sound in the breeze like a wet flag-waving, and then he hit the ground at what seemed to be a greatly sped up rate. The tip of the grenade launcher hit the ground as Buck crouched, reminding him of its presence.

"Thank you, Mr President sir," he said out loud and grabbed the weapon and brought it to bear. There was no way the guy could see what Buck was doing at this moment, but he was approaching fast. Only one chance to get a shot off, he watched the grenade propel itself forward as the rocket ignited and smacked heavily into the Armadillo Brother. He had no idea which one, the rumours were true. They both looked the same which no doubt had to piss them both off.

Flames burst out from the back of the launcher knocking Buck forward. He hadn't fired one of these before. It was kind of scary how easy it was to lob something so powerful; hold the front up, squeeze the trigger on the back and away you go. Nothing at all complicated, and the rocket had already been fitted to the launcher. There was an immense surge of power and a plume of smoke as the armadillo closed in on him. The grenade hit the center mass of the armadillo and knocked him off course.

Buck knew he only had a few seconds to close the distance between them and try to get in there. The gun was useless. As long as the guy was curled up, he may as well have been a rolling rock, but at the same time, Buck was safe until he decided to get back on his feet. The rocket changed the armadillo's trajectory, and he bounced away, clattering into the side of the playground fort as though an angry God had decided to play marbles. The pine timber of the structure groaned and cracked, splinters flying but did not give away. It would probably still take some work to get everything fixed up though afterwards.

Reggie felt himself hitting the side of something hard. He guessed it was the playground. The rabbit had hit him hard, and even through his shell he had heard the explosion. He dared a glance over at his attacker and saw him tossing away the launcher of an RPG. Holy shit! He never had one of those hit him before, and was amazed that he was still standing. Well, still alive. In any case he didn't think he was hurt. Nothing was hurting. But it was still time to get up. He untucked a little, just enough to unfold his arms and get the pistol out and then he started unfolding his lower half, still in a prone position on his back, looking at the rabbit. Buck sprung from the top of the fort, propelling himself down and straight into the armadillo's gut.

The breath was knocked out of Reggie but he still started to scramble to his feet. He didn't have the luxury of time or waiting to catch what was left of the oxygen still in his lungs. A six foot fully armed rabbit, jumping from fifteen feet in the air, tends to do that. He rolled to his side and lifted his arm to squeeze off a round and Buck kicked the gun out of Reggie's hand. Reggie felt fingers snap and he hissed in pain. The gun flew away out of reach, and he groped inside his jacket, taking a knee. Now that he could see clearly, his eyes opened wide. For fucks sake, that wasn't just a rabbit, that was the fucking Easter Bunny! Reggie paused, killing the rabbit wasn't part of the deal as far as he was concerned. He was only there to figure out what the fuck was in those containers and let the March Hare know. His hand flicked forward, releasing the throwing stars he grabbed out of a pocket. They slammed into the pine of the fort. It was his wrong hand after all, he couldn't expect them to hit the fucker. Another thing he didn't expect was that Buck would pluck some of them out of the air, as though they had been a gently thrown balloon, and stood there holding them, staring at Reggie.

Reggie was on his feet now, and started toward Buck.

FACE OFF

'm not here for you," Reggie said between breaths, "All I wanna do is get to those containers."

"Those containers," Buck said. "They're mine. I have no quarrel with you, unless you're going to try to stop me from saving this fucking place from becoming a nightmare of rotting fur, and rancid feathers. Those containers? What's in them is fucking simple, they're filled with guns. My guns."

Reggie pulled out a knife. He wasn't gonna throw it. There was absolutely no point. The rabbit would pluck it out of the air and throw it straight back and even though he was solid muscle, his underside was soft. He'd be sliced and diced like a watermelon.

He made his way past the seesaw as Buck closed the distance. Reggie swung out with the knife. Buck ducked, but came up too soon as the side of the double edge blade lightly grazed through the fur of his face, and he felt a sting as a cut opened on his cheek, little droplets of blood appearing through the fur.

"I'll give you that one," he said. Reggie circled warily. So there were guns inside the container, that made sense. Nothing else really would've been of help. He was pretty sure the rabbit didn't want to destroy the land, fuck, he lived there. Buck looked at Reggie, feinted to one side and swung at his head. His fist connected with a satisfying thud, then pain coursed through it. He'd hit the armoured shell on the back of Reggie's head. He may as well have punched a baseball. Reggie did not even look stunned. A little smile appeared on his face, twirling the blade through the fingers of his hand, as Buck took a step back, and Reggie went past the chains of the swingset following up on his attack. And fell somehow, getting the links of the metal chain wrapped around his neck as a rotting hand penetrated the tree bark below him, pulling hard on his ankle. Buck looked on as, slowly and methodically, a living corpse pulled itself up from where it had settled under the swings, dirt, falling from its body and cascading to the ground below it, spreading brown earth and tan bark. It was like something out of a horror movie, except it was happening right in front of him.

Reggie started to panic. He could feel the hand from where he was being choked out by the chain. He could actually see the thing coming out of the dirt toward him. His fingers couldn't get purchase to unwrap the fucking metal from his neck and he saw white dots starting to appear in the front of his vision.

You've gotta be shitting me he thought to himself. *I'm gonna be fucking choked out by a zombie.* The thing was out of the dirt now. It was missing an arm but that didn't seem to stop it. Lifeless legs slowly extended, bringing the creature to its feet. Reggie could smell the rotten flesh. The zombie opened its mouth and moaned in hunger, its lungs expelling carbon dioxide in his face. Slowly, but surely, it brought its mouth close and snapped its teeth. At the last moment, Reggie managed to move some of his armoured plating in the way of those teeth, and they snapped and broke off against his body. He knew he was done for, the movement had tied the chain even more, and he was gasping and either needed to use his hand to try to push the zombie away or try to loosen the swing. He didn't think he would have time for either.

Opening its mouth now filled with broken fangs, the zombie

lurched right into his field of view as the world started to go black. Reggie found himself staring straight into death, its mouth , a tunnel at which there was no light at the end of. He wished his brother was here. He wished he himself wasn't here. He wished that they'd never taken this fucking contract. The zombie leaned forward, and Reggie closed his eyes, waiting for the pain and heard a heavy thud on the ground and his body went slack.

The chain around his neck was loosened ever so slightly, enough that oxygen was returning to his lungs, and he looked down at the head of the zombie still trying to bite his feet as Buck pushed a machete through it, putting a halt to its movements forever. The rabbit looked at him and lifted the machete up for a second strike. Reggie closed his eyes again, and nothing happened.

"Hold still. This is going to hurt," Buck said. Reggie felt the chain coming off his neck and the world came back into focus. He felt a paw holding his hand.

"Don't touch it," he said, trying to pull away, but the rabbit's grip was like a vice.

"It's not broken idiot. It's just dislocated. I'm gonna fix it on the count of three.. One, two –"

Buck grabbed the armadillo's fingers and popped them back into place. They felt loose and weird, but he didn't feel bad. If Buck had wanted to, he could've permanently busted the creature's hand to the point it could never have been fixed, even with surgery. Reggie looked at him in disbelief. Why the fuck was the rabbit helping him?

STRANGE FRIENDS

As though Buck could read his mind, he said, "You're not my enemy. Unless you make yourself one. This place is fucked, and I really want to believe that you and your fucking brother had no idea what that dickhead had planned." Reggie nodded. That was actually the truth. They had taken the gig, described to them simply as a bodyguard job. This was way above their pay grade, they had performed heaps before taking out elements across the dimensions who had it coming. Nothing like this.

"As far as I'm concerned, we've only got one enemy here," Buck said, "and that's these dead fuckers. Your boss is bat shit crazy though. I'm sure you figured that out by now, and someone else is clearly pulling his strings. The dead are surrounding my chocolate factory and if they do manage to get in there, we are all doomed. The Hare doesn't give a fuck about Easterland. He's after something else that's inside the factory and using these things is just the cowards way of trying to wipe out the problem of getting past my security."

Reggie looked at the Easter Bunny, "You mean this whole job is about stealing chocolate?" He didn't understand. Why would the March Hare even bother? You can get chocolate any where. Buck looked at him.

"No, he's not after the chocolate as you put it. He's after something much more important. He's after what I put IN the chocolate. He's after hope. Hope and Happyness™."

It's the glass and a half that makes all the difference.

Buck went back to the containers. Reggie extricated himself from the chain and watched as Buck punched the code into the second container and its doors slid open with a hiss. He glanced about nervously. It was only a matter of time before the zombies showed up. The thing was, for things that essentially didn't have a brain, they had an annoying habit of showing up when you least expected it and were on you before you even realised that you were trapped. Of course that was only based on TV shows and what he had seen on the news over the last few years. The whole thing was crazy, and he struggled to process it at times.

Reggie rubbed his neck. It was sore from the chain; he'd probably end up with a bruise. Not that you'd see it. Oh well, never mind, he was just glad for the ability to draw breath.

He cleared his throat and Buck turned around.

"I'm Reggie," he said. Buck reached out and shook Reggies non-injured hand.

"I'm Buck." Reggie let go.

"It's funny you know, for the longest time, I didn't think that you really existed. I remember as a kid Mom and Dad talking about about you, but I always thought it was made up to make us behave."

"Well, I'm alive, and I've been around for a very long time, but now is not storytime." He scanned the contents of the container. There were more rockets, which were put into the pack and more ammo. He handed it over to Reggie.

Reggie stood there weighing up his options. With a sigh, he

went over to the other container which was still open and began loading up.

Buck looked at him. "What are you doing bro?" His paw imperceptibly started making its way toward his holstered pistol.

Reggie saw the paw and waved his hand, "No need for that. You could've left me swinging literally when that fucking creepy thing came up out of the dirt, but you didn't so the way I figure it, both me and my brother owe you, and if there's one thing we hate, it's owing anything so yeah, I guess I have chosen a side. It's yours. Let's go and check out the fucking chocolate factory."

He paused. "Do you have a plan?"

Buck looked at him and scratched his head. "Seriously? Do I look like I have a fucking plan? I'm the Easter Bunny."

Reggie smiled. It looks like I can be of use after all.

STRANGE PLAY FELLOWS

"First things first," Reggie said as they sat across from each other on the seesaw. Occasionally one of them would forget what they were doing and tip the other one skyward. Eventually they were see-sawing up and down subconsciously. Buck was really impressed. He thought this guy would've just been a thug. He had heard about the Armadillo Brothers before but of course hadn't taken into account that to be at the level they're at, there would have to be some brains behind the brawn. Reggie continued, well he actually never really stopped, but we needed a couple of sentences to let you know what Buck was thinking.

"You said there is Happyness™ and Hope at the chocolate factory. Is that just a figure of speech or is it actually something that is an ingredient? I can't believe I'm fucking saying this." He maintained eye contact with Buck, who nodded.

"Yep, it's absolutely a real thing. I discovered the formula a very long time ago. We've been putting it in the chocolate ever since. It's certainly not addictive. Well not 100% non addictive, but it does make people feel good." He winked at Reggie, who smiled.

"When you're onto a good thing stick to with it," he said.

"That's exactly right," said Buck, "But in any case, it's also part of the reason why we live so long here in Easterland.

"What do you mean?

"Reggie, no one lives forever, to quote a famous rock band," said Buck, "but people tend to live a very long time around here and it is because of those ingredients that I haven't changed for centuries. In fact the way I saw it was, if I find something perfect, why would I muck around with it and risk the chance of wrecking things?"

"Fair enough," said Reggie. "Continue. So with the chocolate it's got all the normal ingredients that you would expect anywhere in any dimension?"

"The ingredients are essentially the same, but what we do here at Easterland is we add those extra ingredients. That are copyrighted and patented of cour se," he hastened to add. "Happyness™ and Hope, they make us feel good when we're eating the chocolate. But Happyness™ gives energy and most of all helps it taste fucking delicious."

"Indeed it does," said Reggie. I've tried some of your chocolate before, it's off the charts. Why do you only save it for Easter?" He thought about all the money that Buck could've made if this product was available the whole year round.

"Well, too much of a good thing, plus the fact that I've got everything I need. I don't need to be getting people hooked on this stuff just because I need a dollar or two. I'm the fucking Easter Bunny and I think that is part of the reason why the March Hare is so pissed off. I've been here running things for a very long time. In fact the whole time."

"How old are you anyway?" Reggie asked.

"To be honest pal I have lost count. Literally thousands of years old. I don't have an exact number but to give you an idea, a friend of mine, you might meet him one day, by the name of Mike the Alien, nearly caused the space time continuum to collapse in on itself in ancient Egypt when he teleported there by mistake. I was a young rabbit back then, but I do recall being on the outskirts of Cairo as the UFOs brought the building blocks they constructed the pyramids with, and seeing a strange figure dressed oddly, appear out of nowhere. That was Mike the Alien. He was instrumental in making sure the world wasn't overrun with zombies back then, and even now continues to help in the fight against the undead."

"Fucking zombies," said Reggie.

"So yeah, I'm old, but I sure as fuck don't feel it. In any case, the Happyness™ and Hope that goes into the chocolate has an effectt on the folks around here. Unlike what it does to the humans; it lets folks here live for a crazy amount of time which is just as well. That's one thing you get used to when you're as old as me, seeing everyone you love die in front of you and it feels like in a blink of an eye, you lose everything you care about. They live for centuries but even so, it's still not long enough, but it's the best I can hope for. I'm guessing that whoever the fuck is causing this is wanting to get their hands on those ingredients and maybe reverse engineer them for their own reasons. Pretty sure the March Hare wouldn't have a fucking clue."

"I can guarantee that. Max and I... Max is my brother by the way, we were hired to protect him, but to be honest, all he does is sit in this control room in the shopping mall watching video cameras. When he wanted to bring the zombies in we wouldn't help but we stayed because once we take a job we generally don't leave it unless something unexpected happens."

Buck glanced around. It was kind of weird to be sitting in the middle of nowhere, let alone on a seesaw with a grown ass armadillo who just happened to be an interdimensional hitman and bodyguard.

"Do you have any ideas?"

Reggie weighed it all up.

"As a matter of fact I do, but I'm gonna need some help and I think I know just the way to do it. When we get back to the city proper, we are going to have to be careful to avoid some of the camera placements the Hare placed about town. They're not everywhere, but he is keeping a close eye on what's going on, probably to make sure that nothing gets into the mall. To be honest, I don't really think he had a contingency plan for himself for when the place was wiped out. Maybe he thought his employer was going to get him out. We'll need to get close to the factory though to assess the situation. As we saw when you were near the mall, these things do react to sound. We're probably gonna have to pull some sort of diversionary tactic to move some of the zombies away so that we can get in."

"Okay well, let's do it," Buck said.

Reggie started to ease himself off the seesaw and stopped. He looked at Buck and said, "I'm getting off now."

He straightened up and placed his legs on the ground, so that Buck could safely slide off the seat.

"Alright, let's get going." As they walked away from the playground, Reggie reached out and patted Buck awkwardly on the shoulder.

"Thanks."

"Huh?"

"For saving my life."

The two headed back towards town, the factory, and the undead horde that was in their way. *Funny how things work out,* Buck thought to himself. He had thought he'd have to finish this off by himself. At the very worst, maybe Doc Watkins would have helped him; only if Buck could get him out of that damn factory. There were too many ifs in his plan, which really in truth was not much of a plan at all. At least with Reggie by his side Buck didn't feel like he was doing it all by himself. It had been nice to have someone watching his back again. He thought of his family, all of them and sent them all a silent prayer.

HIGHWAY TO CHOCOLATE HELL

"It's not too far to the factory," Buck said, "maybe twenty minutes."

"Twenty minutes of walking feels like fucking hours in this joint," Reggie said looking around. They were just about to leave the paddock area where the playground was. "Either way around, I'm making sure I'm ready for damn well anything," Buck said, popping the magazine from his pistol, filling it with bullets and jacking one into the chamber. He did the same for the machine gun. Every now and then, as he took a step, the end of the RPG bumped the ground. Despite his height, it really wasn't meant to be carried the way he did it. Reggie noticed he was a little bit taller than the Easter Bunny.

"Do you want me to carry that?"

"Might be a good idea, thanks." Buck lifted the RPG strap over his head and passed it to the armadillo who casually slung across his broad shoulders. The exhaust end comfortably cleared the ground which made Buck feel a lot better. He kept waiting for it to hit the ground, ignite and blow the back of his head off.

For the most part, the walk to the factory was relatively quiet.

The one time they had to take any action was when Reggie had to shank a chipmunk that had its mouth full of nuts. It ran at them, its torn face, a grimacing masquerade of cuteness and blood, its chubby paws outstretched from the torn sleeves of its woolen jumper. It lunged for Reggie, who easily stepped to one side and put a blade into its ear, bursting its brain. He gave it a little twist, the sound of bone breaking making Buck'steeth grind. Even in its death throes it reached for Reggie, who pushed it off his blade with a thick sole combat boot.

"Cheeky little fucker," he commented as a lone chestnut finally popped its way out of the zombie chipmunks face and rolled on the ground. It was relatively intact and Reggie picked it up and brought it to his mouth.

"Don't even fucking think about it," Buck said. "The last thing I need is you or your brother turning into one of them!"

"Fair enough," Reggie said and tossed the chestnut away which bounced a couple of times before eventually rolling down into a gutter.

"Better?"

"Lots better. Get ready. We're almost there."

DIVERSION TACTICS

The scene at the factory was ugly. Butt ugly. As far as Doc Watkins could see, there were fucking zombies everywhere.

They were mainly drawn to the entries and exits, excited by the sounds of the chocolate manufacturing machinery. The Doc had been explicit in his instructions that under no circumstances were those things to be turned off, unless directly ordered by Buck himself. And where the fuck was Buck?

You're a poet and you didn't know it. Watkins chuckled.

"What is it boss?" One of the technicians turned toward him, a hopeful look on his face.

"No, no, I'm really sorry I was just having a thought and I laughed out loud. Bad timing. I can appreciate that, let's pan through the cameras again. They fiddled with some switches, but there was nothing that even presented a modicum of hope.

He wished he had the opportunity to study these things a little bit more closely, but time simply did not present itself. He was beginning to wonder; did they contain any vestiges of their last/current previous lives? Some of the behaviours made him think it might be possible, particularly those with not as extreme injuries to their body. To illustrate his point, a gecko lizard in a business suit, who had been aimlessly bumping into cars parked outside, suddenly knelt down, and tied up a shoelace which had come loose. It was a mechanical gesture, the creature did not even look down as it did it, however, Doc Watkins thought to himself, it had to mean there was a little more going on upstairs than they might have given them credit for. He wondered if his human counterparts outside of the forcefield had made any of the same deductions. He doubted it.

He made some notes on the notepad he always carried and tucked it back into his lab coat pocket, then went back to observing. The gecko was back to stumbling into cars, not showing much in the way of brain power. Doc zoomed in on the creature. It had only the slightest laceration on its face and on its tail, which protruded out the back of its business slacks. He wished there was some way he could provoke it into demonstrating other signs of intelligence. Something would come to him. He was sure of it.

"Are you watching the camera?" He looked up, "no I wasn't. Well I wasn't watching what you're watching obviously. What have you got there?"

The Crane operating the cameras flicked a switch with its feathers and brought the vision up on the main screen.

"Can you see it there in the distance? Just behind the factory workers'a car park."

Doc peered closely. He thought he could see something, two figures, moving their way furtively between the cars. One looked oddly familiar. They clearly weren't zombies. They were moving to evade the undead. The profile of one of them was extremely large though, even at this distance and moved with the grace of a ballerina. They were getting closer.

"Well fuck me," Doc said zooming in now and there it was over the top of a car. A set of ears. Rabbit ears. Buck's ears.

"Get me my radio," he said and one of the guys raced away to get it.

"What is it?" said one of the team.

"Seriously?" said Doc, "It's the fucking Easter Bunny."

"Get the rest of the crew," Doc said, "we've got to hatch a plan mighty fast. He looked again at the camera. *Come on Buck buddy. We're counting on you.*

To draw the attention of the zombies away from the factory, the group devised a plan for a distraction. This could involve creating noise or using items from Easterland to lead the zombies away temporarily. Reggie's skills would be essential in executing this diversion without alerting the March Hare or Max.

A STEALTHY INFILTRATION

"Bowl me at them." A statement.

Buck looked at Reggie. He was sure the armadillo would get a head injury somewhere along the line.

"You've gotta be shitting me, like ten pin bowling?"

"Sure," said Reggie, "it'll probably work."

"Great," said Buck. "Are we going to chance the security of the entire factory on a probably? Sounds great! Where the fuck do I sign up?"

"I thought you'd like it," Reggie said. "But no seriously, see that small group of them there? Sure I can roll and curl into a ball, that's what I'm good at, but imagine that same roll powered by a kick from you. Don't worry, you're not gonna hurt me, but it will hurt them. More importantly, it'll draw more over and away from one of the doors. That should let us in."

Buck shrugged. Why did he even give a strong fuck? Reggie was good to go and had already curled up in a ball. Buck almost thought the silly fucker liked being kicked. Must have had something to do with the soccer games that he had heard about. He wasn't sure, but he thought he could hear a slight English accent coming from the armadillo. It was heavily overshadowed by a strong down South tone, but every now and then…

He smiled. *Well what the fuck? The cunt asked to be kicked and Buck was the sort of Easter Bunny that didn't like to upset the children's wishes.*

Hahahah

His internal laughter scared him for a hot second. Then his whiskers wobbled. Danger Will Robinson! Danger! Those fucking zombies were shambling toward them. He thought they had been quiet but obviously not quiet enough. The overwhelming odds of the situation got to him… just briefly and he hitched up his strides and steeled his gaze.

This is serious shit Mr Bunny, he thought to himself. Probably the most serious shit since he'd been paid to put a shroud over the face of a Messiah. That was another story for another time but he was worried that the humans were onto him. Carbon dating my asshole.

Buck dropped onto his forearms and lunged out hard with his hind legs. The muscles rippled and the force of his thrust hit Reggie way harder than he would have been happy with.

Sorry you stupid fucker, he thought but it was hardly enough for Reggie to even register he'd been kicked when he was rolled up tight in his shell. He felt a little push and eagerly he rolled forward. Blindly for sure, but forward nonetheless. It was a game they had played since they were kids. Armadillo bowling. Once their Dad had kicked them out of home, it was the way both he and Max had won enough food to keep them alive. Curl tight and roll like a motherfucker.

A motherfucker who could blink every fraction of a second and alter his course.

Of course.

But no one can talk to a horse of course except for the famous Mr Ed.

Blam!

Buck kicked out and Reggie rolled forward into the throng of the shambling undead. Inside his shell, sounds were muffled, but he could hear the noises of those being trampled under his thick skin.

That little fucker could punt that was for sure. Reggie already knew he liked the guy and was glad that they had an understanding. Buck had one hell of an operation here that was for certain and Reggie wished that he and Max had switched teams the second they got to Easterland. It was so obvious that they had been hired by a fruitcake. He'd seen the carnage out in the human world which had decimated many of the cities. The government had made out that they had it under control but as with anything like that, all it took was one zombie in the right / wrong place and they were back to the Dark Ages.

He and his brother had thought Easterland was a myth designed to keep children happy and well behaved. He had never expected this travelling dimension. He had to help keep it safe, not just because it was the right thing to do but also because it would phase into realities where zombies did not exist. It was a temporal pandemic.

And quite frankly, that would be fucked.

STRIKE!

The first thud made him smile. Contact! The shocked thud of his armored body squashed the zombie he rolled over. Every now and then he peeked out to double check he was hitting dead things and not something random that was alive. Grey brains and pinkish mushy gore told him that he was on the right track. Thud! Thud! Thud!

Squeak!

What was that? He peeked out. Thank fuck for that. An over-turned truck had spilled its load all over the carpark. Rubber fucking ducks. Their little bodies squished under his enormous weight and skipped and sloshed beneath his armor. Splat. Oh fuck that was a kid. Sure a zombie kid, but Reggie had peeked out just before the stupid shit had staggered into the way of his body rolling about.

No time to ponder. Time to roll. The zombies had started to follow Reggie around the carpark, not truly taking in what was decimating them. In truth they didn't even care they were being decimated. They just wanted to eat. Eat.

Brains.

Now that was a piece of bullshit. They didn't just want brains. Zombies were happy to eat any living tissue. It would have made more sense if authors had simply said that they wanted to eat living flesh. Way more sense.

Keep on Rollin' baby.

Breathe in and breathe out, tell me what you're gonna do now.

Keep rollin, rollin, rollin.

Sound familiar? You know you be lovin' that shit right here!

Crunch and splash, inside his cocoon of armor, Reggie couldn't help but smile. He was a force of nature, an aberration of sorts. A science experiment gone wrong. Both he and his brother. On their world talking animals didn't exist and he was an anomaly. Of course that talking racoon had "rocketed" to intergalactic fame.

Intergalactic Planetary!

DEEP WASH

Buck looked on in astonishment as Reggie rolled through the parking lot. He didn't know how the guy didn't lose momentum, but he didn't and that's all that was important at this stage. Zombie bodies splattered underneath him as the armadillo rolled around like an out-of-control wrecking ball. How the world turns, the Easter Bunny thought to himself. He had his pistol in his hand, but he wasn't going to use it as the sound would most likely draw a lot of attention to him. The passage of Reggie's huge body was thunderous enough.

The car park was nearly cleared though Reggie still had a few random bodies to get rid of. His clothes were splattered with gore, but he just hoped that the doc had managed to shut off the main lab. He could see just ahead that the doors were open, which didn't bode well. However, the upshot was that all the commotion outside was bringing the undead sniffing about to the car park. It was in the main lab that the synthesis ingredients for the chocolate were held, and from that point where it was distilled into the main chocolate factory. It was only in this synthesis form that it could be replicated, and from what Reggie had told him on their way to the factory, the

133

March Hare only had the two brothers currently in Easterland and Reggie was certain that the instant Max had seen his brother and Buck together, those tables would turn.

Just when that would happen was another matter though, as he couldn't rely on anyone but himself, his team inside the lab, and, it appeared, the massive armadillo that was rolling around the car park. Reggie was almost finished now. He rolled up to Buck and somehow, Buck was sure it was magic, uncurled and stood up. He was drenched all down his back with blood, guts and bone. It absolutely reeked and Buck wrinkled up his nose in disgust.

"How the fuck can you just stand there?" He asked, "that smells so bad."

"Deviated septum," Reggie said. "I can't smell fuck all." He went to give his body a shake and Buck raised his hands quickly.

"I don't think so pal, give me a second. I don't want to be coated in that shit." He lept back ten feet in a single jump, and Reggie shook. Globs of meat flew everywhere, smacking onto the sides of the walls of the factory, onto car windows, and of course, all over the ground until eventually he had managed to shake off most of the slush. Buck looked around and went over to a fire cabinet on the wall. Reggie saw what he was doing, and nodded as Buck turned on the fire hose and washed down the rest of the muck from Reggie's back and coat. The armadillo nodded gratefully and covered his nose and mouth with his huge hands.

Eventually it was all clear and he shook himself dry. "Thanks pal," he said.

"All good," Buck answered. "Thank you for doing that. It's not subtle, but it's the most direct line of approach. I still think some are coming out however, if we create enough of a diversion, we should be able to sneak past them and get in."

They waited and watched the straggler zombies make their way back out of the factory. Buck was glad that the Doc had not turned on the automated defense systems. A chain gun, chewing through zombie bodies inside the factory would've shut down production for quite some time. As it was, he would have to make sure none of them had got onto the actual floor, where the chocolate was produced.

Buck picked up his radio, "Hey what's up Doc?" He asked, "over."

There was a wait and a silence that worried Buck. "Doc?"

The radio crackled and the Doc's voice came through. "Well Buck that was quite impressive. Your new friend is quite the loco-motive isn't he? Most of our undead friends have left the factory now. I've been able to seal a lot of the doors behind them as they left, but you will still have a little bit of mopping up to do. Would you like me to send any of the guards from inside?"

"No, we have it from here", Buck said. "We may need the guys for other things so I don't want to risk them like this. Actually," he paused. "Get them to go through the rest of the factory, the sealed parts and tell them to be careful. It looks as though this virus can affect any of us so be mindful of some of the smaller folk, including birds that may have dashed through before you shut off the doors."

"Will do," the Doc answered.

"I'll see you soon," Buck said and switched off the radio without waiting for an answer.

He looked at Reggie. "Are you ready?"

The armadillo nodded.

"Well then, help me out with this and you're gonna have as much chocolate as you want."

"What, do you think is the end game? I get the chocolate being special." Reggie said. The Easter Bunny looked at him, paused for a moment, hesitated and realized he would take a leap of faith.

"It's a long story," he said, "but if you like, I will tell you as we make our way through. Let's just say the contents of this factory are some of the most important things ever created. There's even more to it than Hope and Happyness™, and it's not just the Cocoa."

ALL THE SMALL THINGS

Getting into the factory was pretty easy now that most of the horde were scrambled meat outside in the parking lot. Of course they all turned about when Reggie pulled the door shut. It caught on a couple of bodies and made a horrible noise as heads were skinned under the pressure and rasped against the concrete leading in.

Buck was standing behind Reggie as the armadillo used his considerable weight against the door jam but the body parts kept getting in the way. Eyes lolled inside dead faces and hands continued to grab the door frames in an attempt to hold something, anything that might keep them on this side of undead life. The few zombies outside turned with the racket and had turned back to head back to the factory.

Even though they decimated most of the zombies, there were still enough to cause a problem that was for sure. They could not risk letting those fuckers back inside the factory Buck thought, as he pulled out his pistol. There was a weasel skull jammed against the ground and the door, its two front teeth making a horrible grating sound on the little bits of asphalt and gravel.

He looked at Reggie. "Are you ready?" Reggie nodded and tightened his grip on the door frame as Buck squeezed off a round that shattered the stubborn head, blocking their way. Now that there was no obstacle, the door slammed shut heavily, causing Reggie to fall backward, only just maintaining his grip as Buck frantically scrambled out of the way of the armadillo. He was fairly confident he could withstand most things, but he was also sure that cushioning that fall would really hurt. Outside, they could hear feet scrambling and fingers tapping at the door. It opened just a fraction as undead fingers fumbled clumsily before Reggie was able to get it shut one more time smashing his hand across the bolt that locked it in' place. Two dark shadows quickly flew through before the door shut and Buck caught their passage from the corner of his eye. He turned, but it was too late, the little birds flew their way down the corridor and disappeared. Birds from the human world. He had no idea how they would've got through the forcefield but anything was possible nowadays. He shrugged. Let's face it. A truck full of zombies had made their way through so why couldn't a couple of sparrows?

Reggie looked at Buck. "Should we try to get them?" He asked. Buck shook his head. "It should be OK. We've gotta get to the Doc and make sure everything is alright. We have bigger fish to fry, or should I say, bigger Hares to cook."

Reggie's eyes widened and Buck said, "I'm fucking sorry. I know that was in bad taste, just like the March Hare will taste bad once I get my hands on him."

"I'm not going to fucking eat him," Buck exclaimed, exasperated. "It's a fucking joke, a joke! You know, like those funny things?"

Reggie said, "Sure I know what a joke is, but I also know how bad the March Hare smells. I don't wanna be eating anything that smells that bad."

Buck chuckled. "Well, till recently we had a no kill policy around here but now it seems that everything is dead and wants to eat us. Come on, let's go check on the Doc and make sure the factory is not about to burst into a fireball, and then we'll go sort out Mr. Criminal Mastermind."

Reggie agreed. "I'm kind of surprised that Max hasn't seen us by now, but the Hare was pretty insistent on manning the cameras at all times. I just put it down to paranoia."

The two started to walk down the corridor, the same direction the little shadows had flown. Buck hoped that the Doc was OK. He sounded alright on the radio. In any case, he'd find out in just a matter of moments.

WELL THAT SUCKS

Buck pushed the buzzer to the door and the Doc's voice came through loud and clear. Buck let out a sigh of relief. Doc Watkins looked at the monitor that was fed by a camera in the corridor and toggled the switch to open the door. He didn't know who the big fellow was, but if he was with the boss it should be okay. Security leveled their weapons at the door; boss or not they wanted to make sure the big guy wasn't going to act silly. The door slammed open and Doc winced. Buck was always so rough!

"What's up, Doc?" Buck asked and grabbed the human scientist and gave him a huge hug filled with relief. Doc gave the Easter Bunny a hug back and said, "Boss, it's good to see you."

"Likewise, and you guys," Buck nodded at the security team who lowered their weapons as Buck said, "this is Reggie. He is with me. Now, let me know what's going on."

They walked over to a table filled with notes, computer screens and Doc's customary filthy coffee mug, half full of cold coffee. The whole crew gathered around closely. Buck was proud of these animals.

"Buck, the situation is dire. Production has stopped as we simply couldn't keep producing, but not being able to ship finished goods. This has put us behind on schedule and you know, the big day is on its way. The ingredients are currently intact. The undead did not make it past the outer perimeter thanks to the quick work done by Bosco and Shaniqua. Come on guys, let's give them a quick round. They're the only reason we're still alive." There were scattered applause for the two beavers, their fur bristling with delight, making their security uniforms look as though there was a wave underneath the clothing.

"Good work guys," Buck said. "Alright, what about ingredient prime?"

"As per safety protocol, I have destroyed the vats rendering the contents unusable as per your instructions boss," Doc said, "However", he walked over to a safe. "The last backup is still intact." He pulled out a small metal cylinder with a screw cap top. "We'll be able to synthesize this and get us back up and running with only a short delay once you're satisfied it is safe to do so."

"You better get onto it," Buck said as he reached out to check the date on the vial.

"Is this is the most recent?" he asked.

"Yes it is."

"Great. Well that'll be just perfect." Two small shadows darted from the ceiling, one striking the Bunny's hand so hard he loosened his grip on the test tube. The second small shape gripped the vial in its talons, and both flew madly to the door.

"For fucks sake, someone please stop them." But it was too late. They moved too quickly for anyone to react in time to shut the doors, to close anything down that would've saved them. Buck sank to his knees. "We are well and truly fucked. Please tell me you were kidding about that being the last test tube."

HAPPYNESS™ IS A
WARM EGG

Doc shook his head. "I'm really sorry to tell you this boss, that is the very last vial."

"What's the big deal?" Reggie asked, perplexed. "What did they take?" Buck looked at him, his ears drooping. "They've taken everything," he said. "They've stolen Happyness™. If the March Hare gets that, we are all fucked."

Happyness™, the secret ingredient that made Easter chocolate so special, that made you smile, that brought comfort and let you forget about the troubles of the world for a brief moment. Happyness™, the reason why everyone craved chocolate. Buck had been the guardian of Happyness™ since pretty much the dawn of time. In fact, he couldn't remember a moment when he hadn't been the Easter Bunny. He knew a lot of people argued that it was only a couple of thousand years ago that Easter meant anything, but he was more than aware of the old ways, the sacred ways and the rise and fall of the moon had been celebrated a long time before man had ever walked the Earth.

The repercussions of the theft had even more gravity than Buck was willing to let people know. You see, the only reason that Easterland existed was because of Happyness™, and without this secret ingredient being available in commercial quantities, all of its inhabitants, including Buck himself, at least he thought so, would be dead within a few weeks. That's if the zombies didn't get them all first.

Reggie clapped him on the shoulder. "Come on fella," he said. "Looks like we need to go and find ourselves some Happyness™."

Buck looked at him incredulously. "Are you fucking serious? That shit could be anywhere by now."

"Well, that's the thing," Reggie said. "It's not that it'll be just anywhere, I know exactly where it will go and who will get it."

Buck scratched his whiskers, "The March Hare?"

"Fuck yes," said Reggie, "As long as we move our asses, we have a fighting chance."

Doc came forward as did several other members of security.

"Not you guys," Buck said. "You're too important. If we manage to get this stuff, you will need to be ready to start synthesizing it immediately."

"I really wish I had something clever to give you, some kind of gadget," Doc said, looking frustrated but he obediently retreated, and started pouring over his notes.

"Grab whatever formulas you have there Doc and see if you can't make sense of them because worst case scenario, we are going to only have a short window of opportunity to re-create this stuff from scratch."

Doc looked at him. "But there has always been one ingredient missing Buck. I have to confess, I've been trying to replicate it for years, just in case something like this happened."

Buck looked at him with one eyebrow arched. "Say it ain't so Doc, You cheeky fellow."

It was time to fully trust the team. It was against protocol but he had developed the protocols, so it stood to reason he could change them. He took a breath.

"Well there's no time like the present. Here's your missing secret sauce." Buck went to a medical cabinet and unlocked it with a paw print. Inside, he rummaged about and pulled out a syringe and got it ready, fixing a long needle to the top. Then he grabbed a tourniquet and wrapped it around his arm."

"You're gonna have to do the rest Doc," he said. "I can't stand needles."

"Why do I need a sample? Don't we have plenty of your blood in the medical department?"

"That's fine for when I'm hurt," Buck said, "but to do this, you need this fresh."

"Are you kidding?"

"No Doc, not one little bit. I'm the missing ingredient. Take a sample, pull the plasma from it. If you can synthesize the other ingredients, then we're good to go."

"Are you kidding me? After all this time?" Doc said. "The missing ingredient was plasma from you? How on Earth?"

"I'm the fucking Easter Bunny," said Buck. "I get shit done."

"We're still operating on a maybe my friend."

"When was the last time you took or tried to make a sample?" Buck asked.

"About six months ago," admitted Doc, "I kept failing and never thought that this would happen. Well I should've known better."

"Also," Buck said, "it's just over the years, I've never had anyone I could quite trust, but it looks like we're all fucked. If I don't get this stuff in any case, that's the missing ingredient, fresh from the sauce. Pull it apart, examine it and see if you can replicate it in one of those fancy machines you've got out the back."

Doc looked up.

"Yes I know about them. I was wondering why we were able to make so much chocolate all at once. It's way beyond the capacity of these machines out here," he pointed out to the factory floor.

Doc smiled. "I was just trying to help", he said.

"Well in this case, you may have actually saved our skin. Now if you'll excuse me, Reggie and I have a fuck ton of zombies to fight and a dickhead crazy Hare that's bent on taking Happyness™ from everyone in every universe."

"Let's go get them tiger," he said to Reggie.

Reggie took a step forward and then stopped. "I'm an armadillo", he said, matter of factly.

"No shit," said Buck and laughed. "Come on, let's go together."

The pair walked down the hallway after the two flying drones that had long disappeared. "They'll be on the way to the mall," Reggie said.

"Are you kidding me," Buck said. "I went through there earlier!"

Reggie shrugged, "Oh well it's not too far away. Let's go outside."

The sound of zombies had grown louder, drawn no doubt by the cacophony of noise from inside the factory.

"Groundhog Day," said Buck and flung the door open with pistol drawn.

Reggie pulled out a shotgun. "Let's roll," he said. They both laughed.

SNATCH AND GRAB

The Rabbit Hole™ at Marjorie's home sat silent. Max looked around. There was nothing much left of the building. He had known this was one of the Easter Bunny's wives houses, however why she was important to the March Hare, he had no idea. Where the fuck was his brother Reggie?

"I told him to go out to the perimeter, remember?" The Hare did not even look away from the displays he rarely looked away from.

From that point, the March Hare had kept Max busy with jobs that he did not think were that important, until all of a sudden, there was a request that had surprised Max.

"Go to that house," said March Hare, pointing to a map.

"That's one of the Easter Bunny's wives," said Max. "You never told us that we were after the women."

"No, we're actually after the children," said the March Hare laughing, Max hated that laugh. It reminded him of a broken jack in the box filled with glass and bad intentions.

"The thing you're after should be downstairs. Make sure you have a weapon drawn. It looks as though they've been busy." The

March Hare turned on a camera showing an overhead view being displayed by a drone flying over the area. It showed a house partially destroyed with a small group of undead lying permanently dead on the ground.

"Looks like they had a very busy time," said Max.

"You have no idea," said the March Hare. "Now get there and get downstairs. There will be a machine. See if it can be activated and if so, grab the first thing you see."

"What does that mean?" Said Max. He didn't get it. This guy was getting them to do stupid shit all the time.

"It's a portal dumbass," said the March Hare. Max lifted a huge hand and curled it into a fist.

"Now, now, now, not so hasty," said the March Hare. "Remember, I'm paying you well. I think I get to be a little bit rude every now and then."

"Rude maybe," said Max, "but not disrespectful. Reggie and I don't do disrespectful."

"Yes, your brother," said the March Hare. "He's taking an awful long time isn't he?"

"Well you did send him to the edge of Easterland," answered Max. "Who knows what the hell he's had to fight through and we can't tell either, because the cameras seem to go out in different parts of the world."

"Never mind, I'll try to get them fixed while you're going," said the March Hare, thinking to himself, if only you knew dumbass.

"OK, make sure you lock this place up."

"I'll be back as soon as I can,"

"Remember, just grab the first thing that you see in that portal and drag it back through," said the March Hare. "We may need a bargaining chip."

The Hare had seen the footage of his drone leaving the factory. These things were hard to control and had small artificial intelligence built into them, which could sometimes take a while to send them exactly where they needed to go. He had flicked off the camera before Max could see Buck and his brother leaving. That wouldn't do, not one little bit.

Max got up and left, shutting the door firmly behind him. The March Hare pulled the bolt across and locked all of the locks that were still working.

He knew he only had a limited amount of time before Buck and the traitor would show up. He was just hoping that Max would move faster than them and hopefully return with something worth bargaining for.

THAT'S A MESS RIGHT THERE

Max stood out the front of Betty's home. Nothing stirred, and he even prodded a few of the undead with his feet just in case. They had a nasty habit of getting up when you least expected it but normally if you gave them a good kick, they would get up if there was still any juice left in them. Inside wasn't much better, and he could tell that there had been a lot of people making their way through. He sniffed the air, there was a smell of ozone coming from just beyond the kitchen and an electrical discharge smell, as though something powerful had been used, at least in the last day or so. Something too powerful to have been used in a house. What the hell was it?

He went through the kitchen, his huge boots, leaving muddy prints on the checkerboard tiles, though he was pretty sure that whoever was left or came back wouldn't care too much about a little bit of filth. The entire house needed to be rebuilt if insurance even covered that sort of thing? Zombie invasion, crazy maniac in a shopping mall. How would you even put that down on paper for an assessor? You probably wouldn't. He didn't know how things worked in Easterland, but he was guessing that they all just chipped in and helped each other like happy little citizens, unlike some of the dimensions you'd have to work in where every single creature there had to fend for itself.

In the corner of the kitchen, there was a pantry. He looked about hungrily. It had been a long walk out here and he had actually rolled most of it. It was great for speed and great protection, but terrible for the amount of energy consumed. Even one of these chocolate bars they had around here would be great. He opened up the pantry eagerly hoping for some food. But instead, there was a set of stairs leading down to a basement that theoretically didn't exist. At least it didn't appear to exist from the outside.

Max made his way down, his heavy frame causing the steps to creak noisily. He pulled his gun out just in case there was something down there. A heavy blow struck him from the back and he tumbled noisily down to the bottom of the stairwell, breaking five of the steps at the bottom. Shambling down toward him, was a wolf dressed in leisure wear. It stared down at him through milky eyes and attempted to howl through a torn apart jaw, making a gurgling noise. Slowly, it took a step down and fell in its eagerness to reach Max. If it had been a movie he would've laughed, but as it was, Max took his time, took a deep breath and snapped off three rounds. All were aimed at the creature's head. The brain.

They had learned almost to their demise. Headshots were all that mattered to these things. The third shot hit true, caving in the left side of the wolf's skull and sending brain fragments spattering down over the banister to the concrete floor below. The smell was overwhelming; this thing had been dead for some time and Max heaved mightily, discarding his lunch into a corner. The wolf didn't move, and Max got to his feet and looked about.

In the corner of the room, there was a machine with a control panel next to it. Max assumed that this was the portal that the March Hare had referred to. He walked over and flicked a switch. Nothing happened. He moved some more toggles. Fucking hell, he wasn't a scientist, he wasn't an engineer. How was this thing meant to work? He glanced about and spotted a power cord snaking from behind the control panel. It wasn't even plugged in. He chuckled and quickly knelt and plugged it in, flicking the switch on. *Let's try that again*, he thought to himself. The first switch looked like a generic on off switch. The toggle looked like it had something to do with power. He didn't know exactly what would happen other than it looked like a gateway or something like in a science fiction show.

Flicking the button and turning the switch a quarter of the way, Max made sure the machine was powered on and stepped back when he heard a humming noise. As it gained in intensity, there was a shimmering field filling the empty space until eventually Max could see another room.

Strange creatures were there, oblivious to the sound of the portal at their end turning on. There was something nearby. Max turned up the power just a little bit more and the machine hummed. It was a small and fluffy white thing, the image was not clear enough and at this point, Max did not give a shit. The creatures at the other end had now turned to face the portal. They had gray skin and large black eyes and one of them who was now pointing at him, was wearing a gawdy blue Hawaiian shirt, yelling something.

What it was, Max did not care. He reached through the portal, feeling the electrical discharge course up his arm, but it did not burn him. He grabbed the white thing by what he thought was the scruff of the neck and pulled it through and threw it to the ground. As soon as his arm and the creature were through, he switched off the portal with his free hand and quickly pulled the power out of the machine for good measure. He kicked the control panel knocking it loose from the portal itself.

"Who are you?" He said, looking down at what was a rabbit, dressed in a pullover and snow pants.

"I think more to the point, who are YOU?" The teenage rabbit looked up at Max defiantly. "I don't think you know what you've done. My dad is the Easter Bunny. When he finds out you have me, he's going to fuck you up!"

Son of the bunny? Max thought that should do the trick. He grabbed the protesting bunny and shoved him under his arm. Timmy Bunny struggled and wriggled, but couldn't break free. He fought with all of his might until he ran out of strength. There was no point fighting. It was like being in a vice.

"He's going to fuck you up," he repeated defiantly as Max studiously ignored him and vaulted up the broken stairs leaving the house. He had to get back as soon as possible. He had a feeling that all good things were coming to an end. He reached into his coat and grabbed a phone to check on his brother. No signal. The short range radio didn't produce any results either. He hoped his brother was OK.

"OK, little man," he said. "This ride is going to be bumpy."

He held on firmly to Timmy and lowered him to the ground.

"I'm not gonna carry you like this. It would break your ribs, but I will need to tie your hands together." He grabbed some rope and wrapped it around the small rabbit's wrists. Once he was happy with the knot, he hoisted Timmy's arms over his head, putting the bunny firmly on his back.

"Don't even try to get away", he said. "I don't want to hurt you and I'll really try not to but you even think of escaping, I will shoot you so badly that you will wish that these dead things had got you instead." He felt Timmy's arms tense and he laughed. "You obviously don't know about my kind," he chuckled. "You don't have a fucking hope in hell of choking me so don't bother trying. Just hold on normal-like because it's going to hurt a lot if you come off my back."

Timmy held on as Max ran. The armadillo's hard armoured back bounced heavily against Timmy's ribs, which he protected with his elbows. The ache from his Dad's kick reminded him of how much he had lost. The world became a blur as they raced their way back to the mall and into the March Hare's lair.

IT'S A SMALL MOLE
AFTER ALL

For the most part, the journey to the mall was reasonably uneventful. It was, for the most part, fine as long as they stuck to the back alleys and through the backyards of the houses in suburbia. Easterland itself wasn't very big; the size of a small city. There were forested areas outside of the main city, but for a trans-dimensional habitat it did okay.

For some reason when Easterland shifted dimensions it cloaked itself with its new environment, allowing residents to leave the area, and through some sort of magic, Buck really had no idea how the science worked, everyone seemed to make it back in time for the shift. He could've sworn on more than one occasion that some of the kids had gotten out, but the magic of Easterland pulled them along for the ride. It was as though they had been marked as residents.

Then it dawned on him.

Happyness™. It was the Happyness™ that was in everything in Easterland that made them part of what made the place so great. The environment itself pulled the residents along with it, never skipping a beat. Easterland had always existed, but Buck remembered centuries of wandering through the desert, but for some reason, no one ever saw him as a man sized rabbit. They just saw him as one of their own. It was his very magical nature that protected him from everything, but within Easterland, while he did have the upper hand, he was as vulnerable to attack and injury as the rest of them. Well, maybe not as vulnerable, but he certainly wasn't invulnerable like he was on the outside.

It seemed as though someone had cleared most of the zombies out of suburbia. It could've been all the noise made at the factory, the fighting, and the gunshots in other built up areas. He could hear firearms being used and hoped that those lucky enough to still be able to use them were okay. The downside was that the goddamn sound drew these undead fuckers to you like moths to a flame.

Being quiet was the better option, as was steering clear of all the security cameras and drones that were all over the place. It was funny. You never noticed them, they were small and innocuous but now he could see how much planning and preparation the March Hare must've put into this operation.

The drones, of course, that was another matter. They all started appearing after the zombies did, but those cameras could've been there for a very long time while he planned his attack in more than a small way. It was just as well that he was bat shit crazy. But whoever his employer was... That was another matter.

It was kind of weird when Buck thought about it carefully. They had not seen any humans since the initial outbreak; it was as though they had... been removed. Or the sheer fact that they didn't really stand a chance against their animal counterparts. It was surprising that humans had been able to enter Easterland at all, except it made sense if someone had been fiddling with the force-field. Once all this was over, they'd have to have a chat about how that happened and whether Reggie had any more to do with this mess other than drive the truck through.

It wasn't as though they weren't signs of the human invasion. Corpses were scattered haphazardly through the streets and on one occasion, Reggie stomped down hard on a head that was still chattering in a gutter. Buck looked at him. The skull shattered and ooze seeped out from the zombie's eye sockets before the last chatter happened and the thing lay still. Buck looked at him questioningly.

"Some little kid might've put their paw in that," said Reggie. "They're 'alive' until there's brain death. No point in taking an unnecessary risk. Speaking of risks, from now on you are going to be on camera. There is no way around it and that little bastard watches those things like a hawk."

"We just gotta hope that Max is also watching." Buck said hopefully.

"I think he must've been up to something else because if he had seen me on camera with you, there is no way he would be helping him anymore."

"That might be the case," Buck said. "You mentioned earlier he's had something like a secure room he could lock?'

Reggie looked Buck up and down. "Maybe for someone your size though, not with your strength," Reggie added. "It's not like it's a bank, it's a shopping mall. Plus, Max can break his way into almost anything. No, it's something more than that."

He stopped and considered, "The best way in is from the north. It will hem us in a little, but it's the most direct route plus…" he looked around. "It seems as though most of the dead ones have been taken care of. Thank God it's not the zombie apocalypse like in the movies and that us creatures are made of sterner stuff."

SHOP TILL YOU DROP

Around the north side of the mall, that was where the delivery trucks back then had dropped stuff to the docking bay. For the most part Easterland was self-sufficient, but depending on where they materialized, sometimes the delicacies of the local area were too much to pass up, and Buck often arranged trade deals with selected merchants to bring them in. Well, at least to the border where their own trucks would collect them.

At first the humans thought it was odd; driving to a place that they thought was just a road and a weird looking driver would approach them. Cash changed hands. It was always cash, and they would move all the stock from one truck to the other while the human got lunch somewhere. Even if it was only thirty minutes, the truck was always empty and locked up securely by the time they got back. The other truck would always be gone. It was like magic.

Those trucks, though, then made their way to the Easterland Mall, and right to this loading bay that Buck and Reggie were currently heading toward. There was a crush of small vans, trucks, and other delivery vehicles all scattered haphazardly near the entrance as though their drivers had all decided to leave after parking badly.

"Some of that was us," Reggie said, "just to slow down anyone who thought coming this way would be a good idea. We had to make it a bad one."

It felt a little too easy, Buck thought to himself. He scratched his whiskers and rotated his big ears around, trying to hear anything that might give him a clue as to why this place was so empty. He heard a sound that drew his attention: a baby crying. *Why the fuck was a baby still here?* He motioned to Reggie to come with him and they walked further down toward the loading bay. The crying was more insistent now, inside a red car that was also jammed in where the trucks and vans were.

The sound of a baby was very clear. It still sounded off.

Reggie whispered, "That was not us. Be careful."

The red car seemed to be vibrating with the sound of the crying. Buck gingerly opened the door. He could see the baby carrier in the vehicle and something moving under a blanket. He lifted it out and the blanket fell away, revealing the rotting face of a baby piglet. He held it out at arms length, wanting to drop it but at the same time thinking, *It's a fucking baby.*

The piglet riggled viciously in his grasp, snapping its snout vigorously in the direction of his outstretched arms. It moved so quickly that Buck nearly dropped the fucking thing. As he deliberated, he could hear other noises coming from the other cars and vehicles. Then the piglet was ripped out of his hands as Reggie put it back inside the baby carrier in the car and shut the door, locking it with a push of the door button he held in his hand.

"I saw the keys were in there," he explained as he bent down and put them on one of the tires. "Let's face it. It's not gonna bother the thing if the car gets hot. Something for us to figure out…"

A guttural roar erupted from behind them.

A sow stumbled toward them, almost as though drunk, her

house dress ripped to shreds, exposing the rotting and ripped flesh underneath. It was as though someone had taken this housewife, set her down for a fancy mid afternoon tipple, and then decided to rip it a bit.

The speed at which the virus had ripped through Easterland stunned Buck. Whilst the body count wasn't as high as it could have been, it was nothing more than sheer dumb luck that it hadn't been a lot worse. Thank God he hadn't seen any of his close friends affected, though to be honest, he hadn't had the opportunity to check on them. Later, it had to wait for later. The sow reached out in hunger, her trotters extended, trying to grab Buck. He ducked under the swinging arm and kicked hard at one of her legs. Her face smashed against the glass of the car where the piglet still shrieked unnaturally.

There was a sound of tusks snapping and windows cracking.

The sow somehow got her arms around, pushing herself off the vehicle, parts of her rotting face remaining on the glass. Spinning about, she gained momentum, and one of her forearms smacked Buck in the side of the head, knocking him backwards. Staggering, he fell to the ground, dazed. The housewife roared through a face full of mangled tusks and broken teeth. The bristles on her snout spread as her face split into a rotten smile. Scrambling backwards, Buck felt desperately for his pistol which was out of reach. His arms were shaky from the force of the hit and he could not get up.

Well, this is fucked, he thought to himself.

The sow came forward, tottering on spindly back legs, the rotten bloated stomach forcing the house dress to split open. Gobs of mucus and saliva splattered as the zombie shook its head and started to fall forward. Buck winced and closed his eyes as a thick boot kicked the sow in her face, taking off the bottom jaw.

Uncomprehending, the thing looked up, its tongue probing for teeth that were no longer there.

"Get back," Reggie said, and Buck pushed himself out of harm's way. The armadillo kicked out again with his boot, but the zombie kept on coming.

"Not today, pork rind," Reggie said as the thing that had once been a mother continued to scramble toward him, attracted by living flesh. With a deft motion, Reggie slid a hunting knife from its ankle holster, and stabbed down hard into the thick skull of the sow. The blade glanced off, and he took another shot, this time spearing it directly in the cranium. The thing twitched a few times, let out a massive oink, and then lay still.

"That was a good idea with the knife," Buck said.

Reggie looked around and nodded. "I thought so too. Nice and quiet."

It didn't seem as though anyone else was about. The squeals of the piglet continued. *Do these things die?* Buck thought. Surely if they ran out of food something had to stop at some point, or was it simply when they had rotted to the point they could no longer move. Yes, that was most likely the case.

Reggie helped him to his feet. "Are you OK?" he asked.

"Yeah, she just caught me by surprise."

"She didn't cut you at all?" Reggie said.

Buck checked himself over then let Reggie do the same.

"No, you're all clear. Must've been a hard hit though."

"It sure was."

"Well, see that door up ahead where you pointed? That goes through the loading bay. It's the easiest way in there and the mall has been cleared out by myself and Max."

Buck walked up the steps to the thick bolted door. He tried the handle and it didn't budge. Grunting, he pushed harder, and though the metal creaked under his strength, it still did not give away. He looked about for something that he might be able to jimmy into the door, possibly work it a little bit loose or at least loose enough for Reggie to help him rip it from its hinge.

"What do you think you're doing?" Reggie said.

"Trying to get into this fucking thing, what does it look like?" Buck retorted sharply.

"I got this," Reggie said.

Moving back to one side, the Easter Bunny shook his head. "Reggie, you won't be able to open it by yourself. Whoever put it together did a really damn good job."

"I bet I can," Reggie said, gripping the handle firmly. "In fact, I'm so sure I can open this door, I'll put fifty on it."

"Are you fucking kidding?" Buck said. "You want to place a bet on opening a door? Well sure thing," he pulled out his wallet. "I'll take that bet."

"Done deal," Reggie said and pulled out a key from a pocket and slid it into the lock, which made a most unsatisfying click as Buck handed over the money. Then he laughed, "Well played, good sir. Well played."

Reggie put the key back in his pocket and the door opened on well oiled hinges.

"Are you ready?"

MALL RATS

Buck hadn't been to the mall for quite some time. Shopping just wasn't his thing, but occasionally he threw the kids some money to go buy something for themselves or for their mothers. He'd been there for the opening of course, but other than that, only the occasional food pick up, or dropping off or picking up the rabbits.

He looked around at all the broken windows and glass scattered across the polished tile floor. All that illuminated the place was the emergency lighting. It was creepy. Fluorescent globes swung crazily as they dangled, broken from the ceiling, but there was not a body to be seen. Blood was everywhere. But where were the bodies? He looked at Reggie.

"Incinerator. They're in the incinerator. We couldn't believe they kept getting up until we figured out the whole brain death thing. Even the Hare was shocked, at least initially. Then he thought it was funny until one of the dead ones got back up and grabbed him by the leg. Max got to it in time, but it was close. After that, it was all head shots and bodies being burnt, just in case we had missed whatever it is that keeps them alive. Any survivors were chased back outside when the boss wasn't looking."

Little sounds permeated the silence as though the building itself was a living, breathing creature, slowly drawing in the air and releasing it. Each sound had Buck on edge and his grip tightened on his pistol in the darkness. The red light of the security cameras stared at them ominously.

"The Hare watches them all day," Reggie said. "I would be very surprised if he didn't know we were here. He's holed himself up in the security room downstairs. We need to go down the escalator to the left."

The March Hare held the vial tightly in his hand, gradually twirling it about his fingers absentmindedly as he watched the video footage of Buck and Reggie making their way through the mall. Next to him, strapped into a chair, Timmy struggled to get loose. The Hare had shoved a sock in his mouth several hours ago. The kid just didn't shut up. All that needed to happen now was for his employer to come and collect the Happyness™ that he held, then they had assured him that Easterland would finally be his. It had a nice ring to it, the Easter Hare.

On the table was a syringe, its contents murky, the needle exposed. If he got the opportunity, that needle would be stuck in the rabbit soon, the concoction more than enough to take out the bunny and this stupid kid. But not before he had the chance to let that bunny know what he thought of him. Then the games would truly begin.

He glanced at his little drone hovering by, its camera gleaming and an idea came to him. He could actually use the drone to livestream the moment the Easter Bunny became a zombie and was locked in a room with his own child.

Oh, the fun! Then once the kid was dead, he'd have them both put in the cage to watch whenever he played. He needed Max back as soon as possible, but for now the armadillo was patrolling the outside of the building at his insistence. It wouldn't do for him to see his brother, oh no sir. Not at this moment, they were close. Oh so close.

The March Hare knew that in a one-on-one, he wouldn't have stood a chance against Buck, not even with all the fire power he had. The bunny was too strong, and Reggie was too bulletproof. But with the little dip shit in the chair, he had a fighting chance to get through this in time for his employer to arrive. They should've been here already, but it was hard to accurately predict arrival times in a world that literally phased through dimensions and realities.

Timmy was the key to making that naughty rabbit behave.

MAX

Max made his way around the outer perimeter of the mall. Why the hell did the March Hare want him to go out here when the Easter Bunny was so close? He had no idea, but at the end of the day he was here to follow orders. He and Reggie got paid more than enough to do just that. He got out his phone. The stupid thing did not work inside thanks to the March Hare installing a jamming module on the cell tower on the roof of the mall. It had effectively stopped any data reaching him, but if he waited in just the right spot outside, little snippets of data would download. It was sporadic, but he didn't trust the Hare one little bit.

Near the loading bay, he could see signs of a recent struggle and there was a muffled squealing from a locked car. The damn baby. He'd not been able to bring himself to finish it off, even though it was already dead. On the ground near the car was a headless body wearing a house dress. This was new. Max carefully made his way toward the body, knife in one hand, phone in the other.

It was so silent out here it gave him the creeps. It was as though the very air itself had died.

There was a large boot print in what remained of the head on the ground. Max immediately recognizing it as his brother's. He looked around. "Reggie," he called out quietly, "where the fuck are you?"

There was nothing but silence. He hadn't seen or heard from his brother since the Hare had sent him to investigate the containers at the outer perimeter of Easterland. The Armadillo Brothers had made a name for themselves by not asking too many questions.

"Reggie," he called out a bit louder. He didn't want to bring anything else down the loading dock alley; he didn't want to have to fight his way back inside, but there was nothing, no answer.

A whirring noise overhead got his attention and he looked up. It was one of the small drones that he and his brother had developed for surveillance. It was quick, nimble, and even better, kept self charged via a delicate solar array built into its back. He hadn't got a clear signal from it since, well, let's just say for quite some time thanks to the fucking Hare. Maybe he could connect with it now.

Max hunkered down and opened the application that connected with the drone. It worked like a charm and for the first time, he got to see what had become of his brother since he had left the mall right up until he saw that bunny save his brother from the creature in the pit and the two of them left the playground together. His face frowned as he scouted at the footage. Eventually, the video died, but not before the incident at the chocolate factory, where once again, he saw Reggie working together with the Easter Bunny.

The drone suddenly took off, cutting the connection. It was programmed to investigate movement. Max would worry about that later. For now, he had to get back inside. That rabbit had saved his brother's life, and was now walking into a trap. He felt guilty in the knowledge that he was the one who had snatched the kid. He wasn't proud of that and hopefully he had time to make good on it. He was pretty sure that Reggie was somewhere nearby, or had been at some stage, and though, in all honesty, any of the larger animals could've made that boot print, he instinctively knew it was his brother, and now had confirmation on video that, at least twelve hours ago, he was alive.

Max opened the door to the loading bay, locking it behind him. As he started to head back to the security room, he heard the sound of gunshots.

HOT CHOCOLATE

Reggie made his way down the escalator after Buck. He knew how much the March Hare relied on the cameras, and even though the crazy fuck knew they were there, it wouldn't hurt to cut out his eyes a little bit. Taking aim, he shot the nearest camera, smiling with satisfaction as it sputtered and died. Buck looked back, pulling out his own weapon. Reggie waved to him.

"Sorry about that. Should've given you the heads up."

"You're not fucking kidding. Next time warn me."

"Well there is going to be a next time. I'm gonna shoot out some of the cameras. The March Hare knows we're here but he doesn't need to see us as well."

"Good idea," said Buck and stepped further into the darkness below.

Reggie noticed movement above the rabbit and started to yell, "Look out!" It was too late. A large security grill slammed shut behind the Easter Bunny, trapping him inside. Reggie threw his considerable weight at the barrier which shuddered, but did not move. He knew he couldn't get past. He saw the rabbit looking at him through the grill and for once he was sure he could see just the smallest bit of fear in the Easter Bunny's eyes.

"It's okay Buck. We'll figure something out. There is another way in there, but it's going to take me some time. You're almost there. Just keep moving forward and don't forget, where possible, to take out those stinking cameras. You might need this." He slid a pistol and two magazines under the door.

"Don't go crazy. The little bastards got a lot of guns and even worse, my brother might be in there. Please be careful." Buck nodded and made his way into the darkness.

Reggie shook his head, this was not going to plan. Slowly he walked back up the escalator to the floor above. The other entrance to the security room was around the other end of the mall. It would take him a good five minutes even to get that far. Might have to run. His heavy boots started echoing in the stillness. As he reached the top, he saw a hulking figure in the distance. It raised a pistol to the air and shot upward, then pointed the gun back at him.

ARMADILLO BROS

"**D**on't move," a voice Reggie knew commanded. He started forward and a tile near his left foot shattered as a bullet smashed into it.

"I said don't move fuck face." It was Max.

Slowly he lowered himself to the ground and said, "How many times did Mom tell you not to shoot at your brother? It's me, Reggie, dickhead."

He heard Max taking a shuddering breath and slowly raised his head as his brother ran to him and the Armadillo Brothers hugged.

"You silly shit."

"Until two minutes ago, I thought you were fucking dead," Max said, "and then I see that rabbit save your fucking life." He pointed to his phone and brought up the footage.

"How the fuck did you not see that earlier?" said Reggie.

"The Hare blocked any incoming signals. I went outside just then for the first time in what feels like forever and that's when I got this. Where's the bunny?"

Reggie pointed back down at the security grill. "He's behind that thing. The Hare slammed it down when I was making my way there. He's effectively trapped."

Max looked at him. "There's only one other way to get there and Reggie, you're not gonna be happy with me, but I snatched the bunny's kid."

"You did fucking what?"

"I can't say I'm proud of myself, but the Hare told me where to go and there was this portal thing, and he told me to grab the first thing I saw when it was activated. Turns out it was this kid, Timmy. Says he's one of the bunny's kids. Now he's tied up in the security room with the March Hare who plans to use him to stop the bunny from whipping his ass."

Reggie looked at him. "You fucking idiot. We don't snatch and grab kids."

"I didn't fucking know. He said get the first thing you see and I pulled him back. He's a tall kid and he's a teenager. I don't know what the fuck they feed them."

"Never mind, it's good to see you Max."

"You too Reggie. Now let's see what we can do about this hare before Easterland is fucked."

The Armadillo Brothers ran down the mall. There was an entrance down the end of the food court that ran down to an internal alley. At the end of that alley was a small door. Max had the key. Reggie just hoped they'd be there in time.

SECURITY BLANKET

n the darkness, Buck could see that the security room door was slightly ajar. He drew his gun and cautiously made his way there. He ducked as a scrawny paw reached out from the door, firing a shot wildly down toward him. The sound was deafening and echoed off the tiles. Two more shots fired, and he returned his own volley of bullets as he hid behind a trash can. It was thin metal and wouldn't hold up against larger caliber ammunition. As he shot back, the door slammed shut and a crackling noise came from overhead as the speakers to the mall were activated by the security room.

"Let me in, you son of a bitch," Buck said.

"I don't think so, Easter Bunny, you see all I've gotta do now is wait until my employer gets here. I've got all sorts of goodies in here to keep me occupied, including your precious Happyness™."

Through the murky glass, Buck could see the March Hare hold the vial containing the very life essence of Easter itself. He fired a shot at the door but the lock held. Another round and it started to give way. He would only get one shot at this. Buck ran as fast as he could, rolling himself into a ball and smashing through the door.

Springing to his feet, he pointed the gun at the March Hare, who had his back to Buck. Something moved behind him.

"You might not want to do that", said the March Hare. "Always the hero aren't you? But it would be a real shame if you missed me and put a hole in this young man." He turned around spinning a chair with him, revealing Timmy bound and gagged with a syringe full of murky liquid hovering near the young rabbit's neck.

"You leave my son out of this," Buck said as his paw holding the pistol trembled.

"There's an easy way and a hard way to do this," said the March Hare. "You want to save your kid's life?"

Buck nodded.

"Then I'm going to make it simple for you. Trade places with him," the March Hare gestured to another chair nearby, motioning with his gun for Buck to sit. "Oh and before you get any funny ideas," the March Hare said, "put your fucking gun on the ground or Peter Cottontail here might just get an idea that you are good for a snack. Well, after a jabbing with this little treasure."

"What is it?" asked Buck as he dropped his pistol and kicked it across the floor. Slowly he lowered himself into the chair.

"Good boy, strap yourself in," the March Hare pointed to some electrical tape. "And I'll know if you do it too loose. I don't know how long I can stop myself from making little Timmy here into a pincushion."

Buck grabbed the tape and vigorously wrapped it around his wrist.

"How am I meant to do the other hand?"

"You're not meant to, smart ass. Do your legs."

Buck wrapped the tape around his legs, rendering himself immobile. This was not how this was meant to work out. He looked at Timmy who was staring at him, his whiskers trembling.

"It'll be okay son. Everything will be OK," he soothed him. Then he looked at the March Hare.

"Why are you doing this?"

The March Hare placed the syringe on the desk and with the pistol pointing directly at Buck's head, approached him.

"Don't try to do anything funny," he warned the rabbit as he picked up the tape with his free hand and started to strap Buck's free wrist to the chair. Looking at his handiwork, he reversed his grip on the pistol and whipped Buck across the head.

Timmy spat the cloth from his mouth and yelled, "No! Dad!"

A small cut appeared just above the rabbit's eye and blood welled. The March Hare giggled. It was going to be a good day after all.

"I should've been in charge of Easterland," he yelled at Buck, saliva spitting out from between his large front teeth. "It should've been mine, all mine. I remember when I first met you when I was growing up and I thought to myself one day, I'll have that job, but it turns out you just don't die. Do you?" He smashed the pistol again into Buck's head.

Buck winced as he saw the pistol descend on him. It would take a lot more than a pistol whipping to take him out, but it still hurt. Already, he could feel his heart rate increase as powers beyond his understanding quickly knit back together the ruptured skin. The March Hare saw the wounds closing of their own accord and grinned even wider.

"What a cool party trick! I'd like to have me some of that," he leant forward and licked the drying blood off Buck's fur. *It doesn't work like that*, Buck thought. Over the centuries, let's face it millennia, this wasn't the first time someone managed to get their hands on him and do the whole drinking blood routine.

He didn't know why, but it just didn't work. Buck also knew he had never been faced with the possibility of losing something he cared about if he didn't shut the fuck up and do as he was told. The March Hare rained blows all over his body. He kept eye contact with his son. Timmy was all that he cared about. Just get the kid out of this. It didn't matter what happened to him.

"You just don't quit do you?" The March Hare panted, wiping the Easter Bunny's blood off the bottom of the gun.

"Well, we're getting nowhere fast here. Soon, my employer will be here and take the Happyness™. In the meantime though, I get to make my own little Easter zombie. As a matter of fact," he paused and gestured grandly at the two bound rabbits, "do you guys like hide and seek?"

Neither answered.

"Well I do and I have the most fun idea. Now, little Timmy," he knelt down in front of the teenage rabbit. "Isn't it going to be such fun when I stick this syringe into Daddy's neck and he becomes one of the monsters like those outside? And then, we'll have a fun game where Daddy dearest gets to chase you until he gobbles you all up! That's something I'd like to watch. In fact, I think that's something that everyone would like to watch," he grabbed the syringe up off the table and made his way toward Buck.

"You sick fuck," said Buck.

"Now now now," said the March Hare. "Bad manners only will speed up the process. I've heard, and I don't know if this is true, but I have heard that even when you become one of them," he pointed to the security monitors showing zombies massing outside, "that you retain some of what you used to be, but you just can't help yourself. Isn't that a pity? How, just how, is it going to feel when your nice sharp teeth sink into your boy here, and as you tear him apart, a little part of your brain, just a little part mind you, is screaming for you to stop, but all you can do is think of how tasty he is."

The March Hare was positively frothing at the mouth now, excited by what was playing out in his brain. Already, he could see the two of them in a cage as their bodies slowly rotted away. Who knew maybe, just maybe, he would even be able to find the rest of Buck's family and feed them slowly to Daddy dearest!

Timmy started struggling violently to get free of his bindings.

The chair holding him tipped over and the young rabbit fell to the ground, still stuck.

"Good try little shit," said the March Hare. He kicked Timmy in the side of the head. Buck tried to lunge forward, but the tape held. Timmy looked at him for a brief moment as his eyes rolled back in his head and lost consciousness. Buck looked at the Hare.

"Please don't," he said.

"A bit too late for that. I think we've fallen a bit too far down the Rabbit Hole™ now haven't we," said the March Hare. "Try anything and I'll make sure that my next kick means your little boy won't be waking up again. Ever. Not even as one of those delightfully frightful zombies out there."

The Hare started pacing back and forth, clearly agitated.

"I've always hated you. I've always hated this happy place. I was so glad when I was given the chance to take it all away from you, particularly after my own dad drowned at the factory and no one, not even you Mr. Easter Bunny, could do anything to save him. Sure, everyone was sad, and sure you patted me on the head at his funeral but where were you when my mother started drinking? When she started rotting her body from the inside out because she missed Daddy so much! Where were you? When she pushed me down the steps so hard that the neighbors heard and took me to hospital? Where were you when I woke up four months later and Mommy dearest had offed herself in the bedroom because she thought that she killed me? Where were you when I went through the foster system?

Oh, Mr. Easter Bunny, Mr. all powerful king of Easterland, where were you? Fucking nowhere," the March Hare yelled. "You were off making chocolate for the masses. Well, I've never been one to have a sweet tooth," He said, and raised the syringe, ready to plunge it into Buck's neck.

Buck closed his eyes. This was it.

HOLE PUNCH

There was a deafening explosion in the room and he looked up to see a hole appear in the March Hare's chest. The smell of gunpowder filled the room and the Armadillo Brothers walked in, Max still holding his pistol out, ready to shoot again.

The March Hare looked at them. He gasped weakly, "That wasn't supposed to happen," and fell to the floor, the syringe beneath his body.

"Are you okay Buck?" Reggie asked, and then he noticed the boy on the ground.

"Quick, check him." Max knelt down and carefully checked Timmy's head. He gently patted the rabbit's cheeks and stood back as Timmy came to. He looked up at Reggie and then at Max and said weakly, "There's two of you?"

Reggie went over to Buck and freed him. The tape tore off huge chunks of fur, and Buck looked down at the exposed skin. He had forgotten just how pink it was.

Max gently lifted up the chair with Timmy in it and set him upright.

"I'm going to let you out now kid," he said. "I'm not proud of myself, and most certainly mistakes were made, but you're free now and I'm terribly sorry for my part in this."

Timmy looked at him, nodded, and then raced to his father.

"Dad!"

"I'm OK son, it'll grow back," he rubbed his wrists gently and looked at Reggie and Max. "What mistakes were made?" he asked.

"I'll tell you later," Reggie said, "but for now we've gotta get the Happyness™ back to the factory. I think Doc said the latest batch would spoil if it wasn't put in there soon."

"That's right," said Buck.

"Timmy, where are your brothers and sisters? Where is everyone? Are they still–"

"At the North Pole," Timmy said. "That guy grabbed me through the Rabbit Hole™." He pointed at Max who took a small step back. The Armadillo Brother shrugged,

"Look Mr. Bunny, it was a mistake. A mistake I'm not proud of. But I hope that this," he pointed at the body of the March Hare, "makes up for it just a little bit."

"We'll see," said Buck as he pocketed the Happyness™ and made his way to the door of the security room. "Come on, we're going to have to get a wriggle on and it looks like our friends are waiting outside," he said, pointing at the footage of the zombies.

"We'll handle that," said Reggie. "The Armadillo Brothers have got your back."

"Thank you friend," said Buck. "Come on Timmy, we've got to get to the factory and fast. In the meantime…"

Wait, what was that? One of the monitors in the corner of the room had a web camera attached to it. In the shadows, seated in a high back chair, the glow of a cigarette briefly illuminated the face of an unknown person. The March Hare's employer. Buck went to the monitor, glared into it.

"Where the fuck are you? You piece of shit."

The cigarette on the screen lit again and a plume of smoke blew toward the camera. A finger pushed the button on a keyboard in front of the figure. Buck saw the words Mission Failure flash briefly before the connection died. He could only guess what that meant, it was a problem for another time. Easter was waiting.

"Come on son."

HOME TIME

He put his arm around his son's shoulders and they made their way out to the upper levels of the mall. The dawn had just started to break and the sky was filled with pink orange hues but most importantly, for the first time in what felt like forever, there was another feeling. That of hope. Buck grabbed his radio, switched it on, and pushed the talk button.

"What's up Doc?" he said.

A few seconds later, the reply came back, "Have you got it?"

Straight to the point, just like good old Doc.

"Matter of fact, I do. See you soon."

Buck looked at his son as they walked down the street, the warmth of the sun falling upon their faces, even as in the background, the sounds of gunfire and mayhem erupted while the Armadillo Brothers cleared up the mall. *Everything will be all right,* Buck thought to himself. *Everything is going to be okay.* It wasn't too late as long as they had hope and faith in each other.

"Come on kid," he said to Timmy. "We've gotta go and save Easter."

The end.

ABOUT THE AUTHOR

Australian horror author Tory Favro pushes the boundaries of extreme horror from his home base in Geelong. His latest work, "AFLOCKAPOCALYPSE" (2025), plunges readers into a bizarro world where a veteran Diego Cortez assumes the mantel of the Bird God of Death, cementing his reputation for unflinching, visceral story-telling. His earlier works include "Tin Man," a pitch-black comedic reimagining of e Wizard of Oz, and the acclaimed "Little Death Books" series, which pairshaunting illustrations with adult horror narratives. His ongoing "An Other Earth Story" series, featuring "The Dead of Christmas" and "The Dead of Egypt," continues to captivate readers with its unique blend of horror and alternate reality.

This is his eleventh novel.

ALSO BY TORY FAVRO

Aflockapocalypse

Piñata

Tin Man

The Dead of Christmas

The Dead of Egypt

The Dead of Easter

Scrappy the Thug Boat

Lil Chootle Is Off The Rails

The Taxi That Murdered

Max The Pyromaniac Cat

The Good Humored Man

Also Featured in:

Push! An Anthology of Childbirth Horror